7 BILLION LIVES ARE IN DANGER.
13 STRANGERS WITH TERRIFYING NIGHTMARES.
1 ENEMY WILL STOP AT NOTHING TO DESTROY US ALL.

MY NAME IS SAM.
I AM ONE OF THE LAST THIRTEEN.
OUR BATTLE CONTINUES . . .

This one's for Chris, aka Paco Jnr—JP.

First American Edition 2014
Kane Miller, A Division of EDC Publishing

Text copyright © James Phelan, 2014
Cover design copyright © Scholastic Australia, 2014
Illustrations by Chad Mitchell. Design by Nicole Stofberg

First published by Scholastic Australia Pty Limited in 2014
This edition published under license from Scholastic Australia Pty Limited.

Cover photography: Blueprint © istockphoto.com/Adam Korzekwa; Parkour Tic-Tac © istockphoto.com/Willie B. Thomas; Climbing wall © istockphoto.com/microgen; Leonardo da Vinci (Sepia) © istockphoto.com/pictore; Gears © istockphoto.com/-Oxford-; Mechanical blueprint © istockphoto.com/teekid; Circuit board © istockphoto.com/Bjorn Meyer; Map © istockphoto.com/alengo; Grunge drawing © istockphoto.com/aleksandar velasevic; World map © istockphoto.com/Maksim Pasko; Internet © istockphoto.com/Andrey Prokhorov; Inside clock © istockphoto.com/LdF; Space galaxy © istockphoto.com/Sergii Tsololo; Sunset © istockphoto.com/Joakim Leroy; Blue flare © istockphoto.com/YouraPechkin; Global communication © istockphoto.com/chadive samanthakamani; Earth satellites © istockphoto.com/Alexey Popov; Girl portrait © istockphoto.com/peter zelei; Student & board © istockphoto.com/zhang bo; Young man serious © istockphoto.com/Jacob Wackerhausen; Portrait man © istockphoto.com/Alina Solovyova-Vincent; Sad expression © istockphoto.com/Shelly Perry; Content man © istockphoto.com/drbimages; Pensive man © istockphoto.com/Chuck Schmidt; Black and pink © istockphoto.com/blackwaterimages; Punk Girl © istockphoto.com/Kuzma; Woman escaping © Jose antonio Sanchez reyes/Photos.com; Young running man © Tatiana Belova/Photos.com; Gears clock © Jupiterimages/Photos.com; Young woman © Anomen/Photos.com; Explosions © Leigh Prather | Dreamstime.com; Landscape blueprints © Firebrandphotography | Dreamstime.com; Jump over wall © Ammentorp | Dreamstime.com; Mountains, CAN © Akadiusz Iwanicki | Dreamstime.com; Sphinx Bucegi © Adrian Nicolae | Dreamstime.com; Big mountains © Hoptrop | Dreamstime.com; Sunset mountains © Pklimenko | Dreamstime.com; Mountains lake © Janmika | Dreamstime.com; Blue night sky © Mack2happy | Dreamstime.com; Old writing © Empire331 | Dreamstime.com; Young man © Shuen Ho Wang | Dreamstime.com; Abstract cells © Sur | Dreamstime.com; Helicopter © Evren Kalinbacak | Dreamstime.com; Aeroplane © Rgbe | Dreamstime.com; Phrenology illustration © Mcarrel | Dreamstime.com; Abstract interior © Sur | Dreamstime.com; Papyrus © Cebreros | Dreamstime.com; Blue shades © Mohamed Osama | Dreamstime.com; Blue background © Matusciac | Dreamstime.com; Sphinx and Pyramid © Dan Breckwoldt | Dreamstime.com; Blue background2 © Cammeraydave | Dreamstime.com; Abstract shapes © Lisa Mckown | Dreamstime.com; Yellow Field © Simon Greig | Dreamstime.com; Blue background3 © Sergey Skrebnev | Dreamstime.com; Blue eye © Richard Thomas | Dreamstime.com; Abstract landscape © Crazy80frog | Dreamstime.com; Rameses II © Jose I. Soto | Dreamstime.com; Helicopter © Sculpies | Dreamstime.com; Vitruvian man © Cornelius20 | Dreamstime.com; Scarab beetle © Charon | Dreamstime.com; Eye of Horus © Charon | Dreamstime.com; Handsome male portrait © DigitalHand Studio/Shutterstock.com; Teen girl © CREATISTA/Shutterstock.com; Highway 163 Country Road Driving to the Monument Valley © istockphoto.com/gioadventures; Amazing Shot At The Grand Canyon © Andres Rodriguez | Dreamstime.com; Grand Canyon © James Warren | Dreamstime.com; Beginning Of Grand Canyon © Laurin Rinder | Dreamstime.com; End Of Las Vegas © Dmitry Rostovtsev | Dreamstime.com; Las Vegas © Cafebeanz Company | Dreamstime.com; Zoomin' Through Vegas © Kineticimagery | Dreamstime.com; Denver © Rudi1976 | Dreamstime.com; Map Of Denver © Duckpondstudios | Dreamstime.com; Denver Colorado Cityscape © Ron Chapple | Dreamstime.com; Air Vent © Gazza30 | Dreamstime.com; Judo Fight © Jon Helgason | Dreamstime.com; Car Burning, Nightshot © Evron | Dreamstime.com; Lineup Of Sports Cars © Fergy | Dreamstime.com; Sports Car © Zimmytws | Dreamstime.com; Landing On Water © Ander Aguirre Goitia | Dreamstime.com; Flight Controller © Hxdbzxy | Dreamstime.com; Cave Temple, Bhaja, Maharashtra, India © Attila Jandi | Dreamstime.com; Sybil Cave © Leonardoboss | Dreamstime.com; Buddhism Cave © Witthayap | Dreamstime.com; Topolnita Cave © Cristian Tzecu | Dreamstime.com; Taxi © Alain Lacroix | Dreamstime.com; US Marines © Heidival1 | Dreamstime.com; Soldiers Attack © Farek | Dreamstime.com; Hospital Hallway. Internal photography: p102, Drone aircraft © Fabian Schmidt | Dreamstime.com; p113, Washington Monument © istockphoto.com/Tongshan; p163, Security door © istockphoto.com/Florin1605; Danger sign © istockphoto.com/highhorse; p177, Countdown clock © istockphoto.com/Samarskaya

For information contact:
Kane Miller, A Division of EDC Publishing
PO Box 470663
Tulsa, OK 74147-0663
www.kanemiller.com
www.edcpub.com
www.usbornebooksandmore.com

Library of Congress Control Number: 2013946080

Printed and bound in the United States of America
1 2 3 4 5 6 7 8 9 10
ISBN: 978-1-61067-272-6

THE LAST THIRTEEN

BOOK SEVEN

JAMES PHELAN

Kane Miller

A DIVISION OF EDC PUBLISHING

PREVIOUSLY

Sam is gliding high above the Amazon, desperately trying to hold on to the unconscious Dreamer, Rapha, and evade Stella's capture. They crash-land and make their way through the thick jungle undetected, and meet up with Tobias and Xavier, the prized Gear still in their possession.

Eva and Lora continue to be held captive on the luxury boat belonging to the renegade Councillor, Mac. Mac tries to convince them of his elaborate plan—to double-cross Solaris by masquerading as his ally.

Pooling Academy and Enterprise resources and working around the clock, the Professor and the director believe they have traced Stella's location. Alex is dispatched with his mother, Phoebe, and a team of Agents to an abandoned Enterprise site in Vancouver to apprehend Stella.

Unsure about their next step in the race, destiny hands Sam a lucky break, redirecting them to Cuba, close to the location of the next Dreamer. They find Maria, but the recent disappearance of her father means she is wary, and reluctant to help them locate the next Gear.

Sam proves his sincerity to Maria, and with Tobias they begin their deep-sea dive to the ancient shipwreck from Maria's dream. They find the Gear.

Eva is shocked by the sudden appearance of her aunt Julia, who is now working for Mac. Mac takes them to the storage facility in Vancouver in pursuit of Enterprise files. Mac allows Eva and Lora to "escape" his capture. They flee, but remain distrusting of Mac's plot.

While making their way through the Vancouver storage facility, Alex sees disturbing evidence of the Enterprise's genetic experiments. When Stella's forces arrive and start shooting, Alex, Phoebe and their commander, Rick, are separated from their team and trapped underground.

Sam and Maria start a dangerous swim for survival through shark-infested waters. They find Maria's father and Sam is relieved to be headed back to the Academy with his friends, another Gear safe in his hands . . . until an explosive fireball erupts on the road ahead, stopping them in their tracks.

SAM

The firefight erupted before Sam's world had even stopped spinning. The sound of gunshots rang out all around, the echoes washing over them, trapped in the crushed car. Sam reached out to pull hard at the door handle. Next to him, Xavier leaned over to help wrench the door open, but the impact of the crash had bent and twisted the door frame.

The wrecked Guardian car ahead was an empty shell, burning hot and bright. The surviving Guardians sheltered behind it, using it as cover from their attackers as they returned fire. Sam twisted his neck to look frantically at the windows. Each was cracked or shattered. None would provide an easy escape.

How are we getting out of this?

"Out the back!" Tobias called, taking charge as everyone began to cry out and gasp for air. He climbed over to the backseat and maneuvered in between a visibly petrified Maria and her father, kicking open the lift-up door. The other Dreamers and Sam followed. The two Guardians in the front seats were leaning out of their wrecked windows, shooting furiously.

Darts pinged off steel close to where Sam knelt, huddled behind Tobias.

Still crouched and staying close together, Sam, Rapha, Xavier, Maria and Chris all followed Tobias to shelter behind their crashed car. Darts continued to ricochet off the metal frame. The rear sedan had escaped any damage, its Guardian passengers now standing close to the Dreamers on the bridge, defending against Stella's Agents.

From out of the loud gunfire, Sam heard a buzzing noise overhead. He looked up and saw a small helicopter hovering above, rotors blurred in flight.

What the . . ? His fear switched to hope. *Is this some kind of remote assistance from Jedi? That's so cool!*

As he looked closer, Sam noticed that the helicopter had a tiny camera fixed to its underside, and it hovered on the spot, remaining positioned directly above him. He squinted up into the lens.

"Sam! It's not ours—and it's monitoring you!" Tobias called out. "It's relaying your position."

Oh, great. That's so not cool.

Sam ignored the helicopter and scanned the scene, looking up and down the endless bridge highway that stood imposingly over the sea. All other traffic had stopped, turning around where they could to speed away from the fight that had erupted in the middle of the bridge.

Four Guardians were close by, holding back Stella's Agents, shooting and reloading their weapons. Sam knew there were more Guardians protecting their position further up the bridge. From where he took cover, he could see seven rogue Agents, hunkered down around their own vehicles, waiting for their chance to advance.

"Xavier and Rapha," Tobias said urgently, "go with Maria and her father. Use the Guardians' car behind us. Get to the nearest airport and let Lora and the Professor know what's happened."

"What about Sam?" Xavier asked. "We could take—"

"It's Sam they're after," Tobias said, shaking his head. "Go!"

Rapha and Xavier nodded. Sam hastily reached into his backpack and pulled out his dart gun, pressing it into Xavier's hand just before they ran quickly with Maria and her father to the last remaining vehicle that could still be used to escape. Sam watched as they piled into the large black car, Chris at the wheel. The car roared into life and spun around rapidly, screeching down the wrong way on the bridge, back in the direction they had come. As they retreated, Sam could see the car weaving through the stopped traffic and taking the emergency lane to get far away from danger.

Sam could feel the heat radiating from the wrecked Guardian vehicle in front, twisted up against a passing truck that had also crashed in the mayhem, completely closing off the road ahead. The flames mesmerized Sam, putting him into a fearful, almost hypnotic state.

"Sam!"

Sam didn't respond. He continued to watch the flames flicker, his senses all seemingly offline. An explosion of the truck's diesel tanks cut through the air and the hot rush of the fiery wind flooded over him.

"Sam! We're going to jump," Tobias said. "Sam?"

Just like that night with Bill and the fire. I couldn't help him . . . and in the end I can't help anyone, not even myself . . .

"Sam!" Tobias shook him, and Sam, startled, came back to reality. "Listen. We have to jump into the water."

"But," Sam looked over the side railing, "they have a boat down there."

"Exactly."

From his high vantage point, Sam could make out two guys in the back of the boat, manning a rocket launcher.

They're the ones that hit the Guardians' car!

There was one other guy visible, standing at the wheel, obviously ready to drive the idling boat around when the team up top had finished off the job of getting Sam.

"Hide among our enemy . . ." Sam said, starting to see sense in the plan.

Anything to get away from this fire.

"OK, let's do it."

The little helicopter buzzed overhead, shadowing Sam's every move. The Guardians were shouting at each other, coordinating their fire. Tobias called out commands to the closest one who nodded and relayed the information to his colleagues. Then, while the two front Guardians kept shooting at Stella's Agents, the rear Guardians both turned around in unison, the small helicopter in their sights. They each pulled their triggers in the same instant, hitting the remote-controlled vehicle and sending it spiraling to the ground. Sam jumped out of the way as it crash-landed just where he had been crouched. With a swift kick, he sent it sliding across the road into the fiery furnace of the burning wreck.

"Follow me!" Tobias said, running to the guardrail of the bridge and vaulting over the side. At that same moment the Guardians began firing even faster and more relentlessly at their enemies.

Sam followed, hitting the railing at the same spot and hurdling over it—one giant leap straight ahead, without even looking down until he was flying over the edge.

Oh mannnnnn!

Sam flew through the air, his arms and legs thrashing around as though he was still running. As he fell towards the water, he saw Tobias directly below him, a few seconds ahead.

More alarmingly, he also saw the boat directly below them both.

Sam adjusted his Stealth Suit so that the material between his arms and body formed the wing-suit he'd used before. It caught at the air and, with the added wind resistance, Sam adjusted and slowed his fall. He was still headed for the boat but was slowing, gaining enough time to better position his landing.

THUD!

He hit hard, landing directly on top of the guy loading the rocket launcher. The rogue Agent was knocked out cold, and the rocket he was holding clattered to the deck with a loud metallic *CLANG* that made Sam freeze in anticipation of what was coming.

But there was no explosion—the rocket didn't go off.

The other Agent turned around, momentarily caught off guard at the sight of his buddy on the ground and a new passenger standing next to him.

"OOMPH!" he exclaimed as Sam fly-kicked him, sending the Agent overboard.

The Agent behind the wheel at the front of the boat heard the loud splash and turned around to face Sam. His eyes were cold, a smirk starting to form on his lips. He reached for the holster on his hip and then raised his dart gun at Sam—

WHACK!

The guy's eyes rolled shut, and he slumped forward to the ground. Tobias seemed to materialize out of nowhere, the life ring he used to hit the Agent over the back of the head with still held tightly in his hands.

"You drive the boat," Tobias said to Sam. "I'll use that launcher to even out the odds for our friends up there."

Sam rushed forward and grabbed the controls of the

boat, easing the throttle while turning the wheel. He brought the boat around fast to face the bridge.

WHOOSH!

Sam watched a rocket streak up and explode just behind Stella's men, forcing them to run for cover.

SAM'S NIGHTMARE

The sunlight flickers off the water and illuminates the scene before me. I'm standing at a fork in a river at the base of a vast stone wall—not man-made, but a cliff. It is so big. It looks tall enough to be holding up the sky above me.

I've seen this before, been here with my family.

The Grand Canyon.

But not like this. Not from down almost inside one of the massive side canyons.

And I'm not alone.

"This is Cody, do you copy?" I turn to see a guy about my age, tanned and fit, working a radio.

Cody, gotcha.

He tries the radio call again, and again, then switches it off. He says to me, "Radio hardly ever works in these canyons, not this far into no-man's-land. Guess we're on our own."

"No-man's-land?"

Beyond him I see our two kayaks. One of them is broken, cracked through the middle with a chunk torn out and there are no paddles to be seen.

"Don't worry, I've been in worse situations," Cody says, grinning. "Last spring, we had this flood come through when I was spelunking the Getzler Pass. *That* was bad."

"Spelunking?"

"Yeah, caving—you know, exploring in caves?" Cody explains. "That time, it was like being spat out of a washing machine on spin cycle, and I was washed ashore with nothing but the shirt on my back. And I mean *nothing*—I had to make my shirt into a makeshift pair of shorts. Anyways, I got out of there. Took me two weeks, though."

"Two weeks?" I ask, looking around at the red rock walls that reach up to the bright-blue sky.

How do we get out of here? Swim?

"How'd you survive two weeks?"

"Lived off the land," Cody replies. "Swam, hiked and climbed my way to a road."

I look at the river that splits in two at the rocky shore that we are standing on. The water is running fast, foaming white where it collides with rocks. "Lived off the land? What, you caught fish and stuff?"

"Ah, yeah," Cody chuckles. "I caught fish, with my imaginary fishing gear. Made some real nice sushi."

Gee, sarcastic much? What's with this guy?

He walks over and stops next to me, and looks up at the canyon wall. "Incredible, isn't it?"

"Yep."

"They must have been geniuses . . ."

I turn to Cody. He's looking up at the rock wall, staring at it in awe.

Then I see it.

This isn't just a canyon wall.

Someone was here, a long time ago . . .

"Isn't it awesome?!" Cody shouts. "You OK?"

"Er, sure . . ." I hang on for grim life. Below me is an immense drop, spanned by an uneven, narrow rock bridge. We are in the heart of a cave, underground, but I can see a fast-moving river in the darkness. The weak light of my flashlight beams over it and I can see that it's running fast. I can *hear* it—the phenomenally powerful roar of an immense volume of water moving at speed. The opposite bank is too far away to see in the dark.

"We have to cross it!" Cody shouts over the noise.

I turn and shine the flashlight back the way we've come, all the twists and turns and levels that we've descended are now covered by complete darkness.

'You're sure about this?" I ask.

'We're almost there," Cody replies. "We just have to cross it."

I can make out the mural-covered wall behind us, scrawled with scripture in a language I've never seen. The pictograms look similar to Egyptian hieroglyphs, only these are . . .

"Ah!" I say, startled as I bump into the back of Cody.

"Careful!" Cody is putting himself into a climbing harness.

"Why'd you stop?"

"Because of that." He points at a giant cave spider. "It's a pussy cat but you don't want to get too close," Cody says, grinning. "And trust me, you do *not* want to fall into this river."

"You've fallen in before?" I say.

"Yep," Cody says, shivering at the memory. "First time I came down here."

"How'd you get out?"

"Swam."

I look out at the empty black space. "To where?"

"To the other side . . . well, the torrents kind of spat me out over there. Dumb luck more than anything else. It's a long way over too—see how strong that current is? I just made it before the river disappeared into the cave. Heads underground way up that way." Cody's flashlight beam followed the raging river.

"I guess you're a strong swimmer," I say. I follow Cody's lead and take a climbing harness, slipping my legs through and then fastening it tightly around my waist.

"Nup. Like I said, I got lucky, that's the only way I can explain it."

"What's on the other side?"

"What we came for."

"How do we get over there?"

Cody points above us.

"We go *up*."

I look to where he is shining his light.

You've got to be kidding me!

I strap onto the zip line and hang on, traveling blindly through the complete darkness.

When did Cody say to apply the brakes?

Ahead, a tiny light appears in the distance—Cody's flashlight. I squeeze the apparatus that connects me to the line and feel myself slowing, hearing the friction. Despite hitting the brakes, I stop hard and fast when Cody catches me at the end of the line. I unclip and climb with Cody down to floor level, which is paved with smooth stone slabs.

"This is . . ."

"Vast? Incredible? Out of this world?"

"All of the above . . ." I say as the two of us walk up the stairs to a paved ancient plaza. A magnificent shrine made of the same smooth stone blocks stands in the center, surrounded by smaller outer structures. "A pyramid? In North America?"

"I know," Cody says. "At first I thought it was Mayan, but it's not. Sides are too smooth."

"Looks more Egyptian."

"We're a long way from Egypt."

"We're a long way from anywhere . . ." I say, walking towards the shrine. I stop at a large altar.

"Ah, Sam . . ."

"Just a sec." I reach forward, and my hand hovers near an intricate carving. It seems familiar.

I stare at the twelve figures depicted in the circle, focusing on the thirteenth standing in the middle of them, his arms outstretched. It is carved in the stone, but the middle man seems to be gilt in gold.

"Sam, I don't think you should touch that."

"One moment," I say, my fingers inching closer and then touching the little golden statue. The figure feels electric to the touch, and I push against it more firmly—

The figure pops out, revealing itself as a handle of some sort.

"Sam!" Cody whispers. "Listen!"

I freeze, listening. Footsteps. The sound of the river fades to silence.

I turn around slowly. Cody is looking deep into the shadows from where we've come.

Then there's a new sound.

Chuckling. Then clapping.

"Sam . . ."

That voice. Deep, metallic. So predictable now, but always still a shock.

Solaris.

"No matter where you are . . ." Solaris says, stepping out from the dark into the light from our flashlights. "I will always find you, Sam . . . anywhere, anytime."

I look to Cody again, who seems frozen in fear.

No . . .

I reach out to touch my friend, tapping him on the shoulder. He is frozen in time. The river has stopped, completely suspended in motion.

Just like in the cafe in New York.

It's OK. I'm in a dream.

I can control it.

"Sam . . ." Solaris says, his voice sounding as if it is wrapped around a smug smile. "You really think that *you* can control this?" Flames dance at his wrists, making me squirm. "You think *you're* the master of your dreams . . ?"

Wake up!

I hold my hands over my ears to stop the voice from cutting into my brain. I shout at him, "I don't have it! You're wasting your time!"

"You think this is only about the Gears?" Solaris says.

Wake up! Now!

"Sam, Sam, Sam . . . you have so much to learn," Solaris chuckles. "It is so easy to get to you, to feed on your fears."

WHOOSH!

Fire shoots over my head. I flinch and cower to the ground.

"Ha, ha, HA!" His laugh echoes around the cave, deafening me.

Wake up . . . wake up . . . wake up . . .

"Thank you, Sam," Solaris says. "For yet again showing me where I have to go."

Come on, Sam, you're dreaming, you have to—

WHOOSH!

The fire washes over me and I put my arms over my face to shield myself as the searing heat consumes me, leaving me—

Broken.

SAM

BEEEEEEP!

Sam's eyes flew open and his gaze swung around wildly, searching for the danger that was always there. Instead of fire there were bright blinding lights that cut through the night. A loud horn blared as an oversized truck rumbled past, its sound deep and rousing.

I'm OK, I'm OK. I'm in a car . . .

"Hey, sleepyhead . . ." Tobias said gently. "It's all right, Sam, you're with me. It was just a dream."

"What about everyone else?" Sam stammered, trying to focus. His mind swam with images of Rapha, Xavier and the others fleeing from Stella's Agents on the bridge in the Florida Keys, of being on the boat with Tobias, and the rocket launcher that had saved the day. "Are they—"

"Don't worry," Tobias interrupted. "They're fine. I checked in and they're already on their way back to the Academy."

"Oh wow, that's good news," Sam sighed. "And where are *we*?" he asked, sitting up, groggy, finally rubbing the sleep from his eyes. He was bathed in sweat. They were in a sedan, driving on a highway through the darkness. Sam was so disoriented by the impact of his nightmare, it took him a moment to remember the previous day—abandoning the Agents' boat at the wharf and continuing their trip in a rental car.

"Just coming up to Amarillo, Texas," Tobias said. "We'll stop for a bite and call the Academy again, refuel the car . . . and me."

"And me!" Sam's stomach rumbled to accentuate the point.

"Then we start heading north, up to Wyoming and Montana, right on through to Washington State."

"And on to Vancouver," Sam said, remembering their objective.

Lora and Eva were last spotted there and we have to help them—rescue them first, then find the Dreamer.

"Back to our old hometown."

Tobias nodded and yawned.

He's been driving nonstop while I've been sleeping.

"Maybe we should stop someplace for longer," Sam said. "So you can rest."

"I'm good, I can keep on driving," Tobias replied. "I'll take power naps at truck stops as I need them. I'd feel safer if we kept moving."

"No one's followed us?" Sam checked over his shoulder and out their rear window. It was impossible to tell if any of the headlights were sinister or not.

Tobias' eyes flicked to the rearview mirror. "Nope."

"I can drive, you know," Sam told him.

"*You* can drive?" Tobias said. He yawned again.

"Yep."

"You're fifteen."

Sam nodded, before adding, "Well, I can't drive, you know, *officially*. But Bill's uncle let us drive on the farm all the time—an old pickup, the tractor, quad bikes . . ."

"Well, there you go," Tobias said, looking more awake with the news. "That's something I never knew about you. Interesting—and *illegal*, I might add."

"Great, I can save the world but I can't drive a car . . ." Sam smiled and then looked wistfully out his window, memories of his old schoolmate Bill prompting thoughts of his former life. "Hey, you always knew that my parents were Enterprise Agents, didn't you?"

Tobias nodded.

"Think they're still in Vancouver?"

"I don't know, I'm sorry," Tobias said. He glanced over to Sam. "Why? Do you want to find your parents? Have you asked the director about them?"

"Yes, no, I mean, I haven't asked yet. I think I was afraid to. Alex has been with his mother this whole time, but no one ever mentioned my parents so I figured it was better not to know if they didn't want to see me or something. But I . . . I'd like to know," Sam said. "I mean, you know—if they were, well, if they really think of me as their son . . ."

They drove on in silence for a few minutes. There was the faintest glow of sunrise sneaking up behind them.

Sam checked his watch—it was almost five in the morning. "You drove right through the night," he said. "You must be tired."

"Yes," Tobias replied, "we've been driving about twelve hours, but I'm OK."

"Where are we again?"

"Pulling into a gas station," he said, turning off the highway.

"I mean—"

"Amarillo, Texas. I grew up around here." Tobias parked the car in front of an all-night diner and killed the engine. "Come on, let's get breakfast. And some coffee."

Sam got out into the crisp morning air, self-consciously holding tight to his backpack containing Rapha's and Maria's Gears. Tobias walked into the diner. Sam looked around the lot, empty but for a couple of big trucks, then back at Tobias who took a seat in the booth by the big glass window and waved at Sam to join him. Sam smiled and nodded. He caught his reflection in the windows as he stopped for a massive truck driver coming outside. His image was puny in comparison.

And I'm the last hope for humanity?

Sam sighed and pushed open the diner door.

04

ALEX

"It's been quiet for a while," Alex said.

"Too quiet," Phoebe said.

Alex watched as their commander, Rick, pressed his ear to the door, waiting for some sound.

They sat in a locked room in the underground complex of the abandoned government facility in Vancouver.

"The government really was part of this?" Alex asked. "They allowed this to happen?"

"Yes," Phoebe replied. "This site was part of an old program run by the US government before it was shut down along with sites in Australia, the UK and Hong Kong. Their combined research ended up going to the private company that took over when the government pulled out—the Enterprise."

"Hmph," Alex said. "You think they're still out there?" he asked, referring to Stella and her men.

"It's possible," Phoebe said. "How's the arm?"

"Fine," he replied, looking down at the makeshift splint on his busted forearm. "Wish it had been a bigger cut, something to leave a real scar."

"What?"

"It'd be cool."

"A huge scar would be cool?"

Alex nodded. His mother shook her head.

"So," Alex said, getting to his feet and working out the cramps from sitting on the cold tile floor. "How *do* we get out of here?"

"The way we came is the only way in or out," Rick said. "We gotta sit tight until someone comes to get us."

Alex went over to the heavy steel blast door that had shut them into the labs when they disabled the mechanism. It had seemed like a good idea when they were being chased by men with guns. Now it was a prison of their own making. He rummaged through the abandoned scientific instruments strewn across the desks around them—test tubes, Bunsen burners . . .

Aha! So they must also have something to light these.

He began pulling open drawers, one after another, until he found a pack of matches.

"Eureka!" he said.

"Great," Phoebe said. "We can start a fire. Cook up some textbooks."

"Mom, please, don't mention food." Alex groaned in protest, his stomach grumbling as he lit a match. The flame flickered and danced. He could see it was being pulled and pushed ever so slightly by an imperceptible breeze. "Mom, look . . ."

Alex held up the match. He walked around the room, until he was standing closer to where the breeze was strongest against the tiny flame.

"Alex!" she said, getting to her feet. "You're a genius."

Alex walked around a tall set of cabinets and then, lighting another match as the first died out, saw where the air was coming from—a huge grill set into the roof.

"An air vent!" Alex said. "And where there's air . . ."

"There's a way out!" Phoebe said. "But we can't scale a vertical air shaft without climbing gear."

"Leave it to me, Mom, leave it to me."

SAM

Sam joined Tobias in the roadhouse diner and they ordered breakfast. The friendly waitress brought Tobias the first of his bottomless cups of coffee as Sam gulped down a large glass of water.

"Wow," Sam said, wiping his mouth after refilling his glass for the third time. "I didn't realize how thirsty I was."

Tobias smiled. "So, want to tell me about your dream, the one you had in the car?"

"Do we have to talk about it now?" Sam asked.

"You tell me. Do we have to?"

Sam was silent, then sighed. "Yeah, we do."

He looked out the window, into the lonely parking lot, reluctant to delve back into the details of his latest terrifying encounter with Solaris.

"You know, these Gears," Sam said, nodding towards his backpack beside him, "they make them worse—the nightmares, I mean. It feels different when I dream, like they supercharge everything I'm seeing."

Tobias nodded. "That's consistent with what we have been noticing at the Academy. Being close to the Gears seems to have a strong impact on the dreams of the last 13 Dreamers. And, like all of this, I'm sure it affects you most profoundly of all."

Sam rolled his eyes and said, "Great."

"Just imagine being on the other side of all this," Tobias said, sipping his coffee. "When we've found all the 13. When we've built da Vinci's Bakhu machine, putting all the Gears together in the right order. When this amazing machine has led us to the Dream Gate that Ramses controlled . . ."

"*If,*" Sam challenged. "*If* we find all the 13. *If* we get all the Gears."

"Sam," Tobias said kindly, "you must stay hopeful. Hope is our best ally of all."

Sam looked at his old teacher, always trying to help, to keep Sam safe and on track and . . . happy. Finally, Sam pushed his glass away. "All right, then—*when* all that happens, that's going to be a pretty good day."

Tobias laughed.

"Though I'll probably have to go back to school then, right?"

Tobias laughed again. "You *like* school."

"Well, yeah, I guess."

Tobias smiled as the waitress brought their order.

Sam watched her walk back across the diner and glanced at the other people around them.

"Do you think Solaris is a man?" he asked suddenly.

"A man?" Tobias raised an eyebrow. "What do you mean?"

"Well, a man or a woman, but I mean, a *person*."

"Yes, of course I do. I don't think Solaris is some mythical creature or some kind of robot. I think behind that mask is someone as real as me and you, acting out their part of the prophecy and somehow linked to the 13 via your dreams. Perhaps they are pure evil, but perhaps not. My experience of the world tells me that too much power can change who someone is, even those with the best intentions."

"You think you could go all Solaris on us?" Sam said, trying to lighten the mood again.

Tobias smiled, sipped his coffee, kept watch out the window. "It doesn't take much for good people to do bad things."

Sam stared at his breakfast, the words rolling around in his head. Then he said through a huge mouthful, "Is anyone looking?"

"Huh?"

Without warning, Sam changed his Stealth Suit to resemble the hoodie and jeans he'd last worn in New York. Tobias looked around—the few truckers and early morning travelers sitting in booths and at the counter didn't seem to notice the sudden transformation.

"Sam, we are trying to remain inconspicuous. You have to be careful in public," Tobias said, his own Stealth Suit changing appearance ever so slightly from a charcoal colored T-shirt under a dark-green wool cardigan to a black T-shirt and a dark-blue cardigan.

"Wow," Sam said with mild sarcasm, "you're such a daredevil."

Tobias' T-shirt changed to a vivid yellow-and-purple tie-dye and they laughed. Then he changed it again, this time to one with a lame science joke on it:

WHY CAN'T YOU TRUST ATOMS?

BECAUSE THEY MAKE UP EVERYTHING

"Really?" Sam said.

"Not funny?"

"No. Not even on the Tobias Cole lame-joke scale."

"You should have paid more attention in science class, then you'd get it," Tobias said, chuckling. "Anyway, enough distractions. Shall we discuss your dream?"

Tobias' phone began to vibrate on the table between them, the screen showing the name of the caller: LORA. Before answering the call, Tobias plugged in earphones and passed one of the earpieces to Sam.

"Lora!" Tobias said quietly. "You OK?"

"We're fine," she replied. "And we've got news."

"Where are you?"

"Seattle."

Sam looked to Tobias, both of them realizing their road trip had just been rerouted.

"We had to leave Vancouver," Lora explained. "It wasn't safe to stay there."

"OK," Tobias said. "We're on our way."

"What? Where are you?" she asked.

"Texas," Sam replied, "headed overland to you."

"No need. We've got a Guardian flight touching down here in a few hours to take us back to the London campus," Lora said. "We can fly to you, pick you guys up. Sam, have you had your next dream?"

"Yes," Sam said, to both of them. "I was somewhere in the Grand Canyon National Park, with someone called—"

"Don't say any more over the phone," Lora said. "But from what you just mentioned, you should stay in the US and not travel back to London with us. Seems the next Gear is near."

"Agreed," Tobias said, "but we'll need a dream machine to get every detail."

"I can have Guardians bring one to your location, they're probably six hours away," Lora said.

Tobias looked at Sam over the table and a smile formed in his eyes.

"You know what, I can do one better than that," Tobias said, as though a realization had given him a jolt of energy. "I've got the perfect place to go. We've got this—call us when you get back to London."

"OK," Lora replied, her voice a little unsure even though she trusted Tobias. "I'll have a Guardian team on standby at the Dallas airport to hang tight with a helicopter, ready when needed."

"Sounds like a plan," Tobias said.

"Lora," Sam said before the call was ended. "Can I speak to Eva?"

"She's asleep," Lora said. "We're in a hotel right now, and she crashed as soon as her head hit the pillow."

"OK, next time."

"Talk soon and good luck," Lora said, ending the call.

"So," Tobias said, eating his breakfast, "think you're OK to drive on dirt roads?"

EVA

Eva woke with a sigh and a stretch, sitting up in bed and rubbing her eyes. Lora was sitting on the end of the other bed in the hotel room, watching the news.

"Hey there," Lora said. "Sorry if I woke you."

"It's fine," Eva said. "I was sleeping like a log. You can turn the TV up if you want."

Lora bumped up the volume. A story was running on CNN about climate change, with politicians debating whether taxes would curb pollution.

"I don't know why they don't just leave the whole climate debate out of it," Lora said, watching the world leaders walking out of a summit meeting. "Just keep it simple, you know? If you pollute the world, you pay. That'd clean things up."

"Yeah, makes sense," Eva said, padding over to the coffeemaker. "Maybe after this race, that can be our next challenge—trying to convince some of *these* people." She jabbed a thumb in the direction of the TV.

"Perhaps," Lora replied and smiled at the thought. "Did you dream just now?"

"A little," Eva said. "A nice one actually, about my parents."

Lora nodded. "Would you like to see them?"

"Can I?" Eva asked. "I mean, after I learned that they were only my surrogates—you know, Agents of the Enterprise—I kind of assumed that I'd not see them again."

"Most of the surrogate parents are still dedicated to the Enterprise, though a few went over to Stella's side, brainwashed by her crazy promises of giving them more power, no doubt," Lora replied. "Your parents didn't— they're still at your old home."

"Wow, really? It never occurred to me they'd still be there. Have you—have you spoken to them?"

"No," Lora said, "but the director has sent you this." Lora handed Eva her phone, pressing "play" on a video message. It was her parents. Eva almost dropped the phone in shock.

"Hi, darling Eva!" her mom said.

"Hi, chicken!" her dad said. "We hope you're well."

"We miss you."

"We're . . . we're sorry that you found out about things the way that you did. We've been so worried about you."

"But now we've heard you're OK."

"We miss you and want you to know that there's a loving home here for you whenever you need or want to come back."

"We know you probably have questions, which we're happy to answer."

"We love you."

"Panther misses you too!"

"Be careful—and call us if you want to talk. We're so proud of you."

Her mother looked tearful as her parents waved and the message ended.

That was so weird. What a mind trip. Talking to me as if all of this is so normal. I guess it is normal for our family . . . now.

"What should I do?" Eva asked, searching Lora's face for some reaction.

"What do you want to do?" Lora asked carefully.

"I'm not sure." Eva handed the phone back. Her mind was racing, feelings of anger and betrayal swirling around with the love and loss she still felt about her parents and her old life. She missed her home, her friends—and them. "What are our plans now?"

"We're going to head back to the Academy in London to help out there," Lora said. "I could see if we can arrange for your parents to visit us in London, if you'd like."

"You think it would be dangerous for me to visit home? Even though we're close now?"

"I'm sorry, but yes, I do," Lora replied. "There are more than a few people who think you will be one of the last 13, Eva. It would be better if you had them come to the Academy, where it's safer."

Eva frowned, staring absently ahead.

"Eva? What is it?" Lora's concern was obvious.

Something's not right.

"What they said before, about Panther missing me too," Eva said.

"Who's Panther?"

"My cat."

"Well, he probably does miss you," Lora said.

"No, not likely," Eva said, feeling a rush of heat around her neck as she broke into a worried and nervous sweat. "He's dead. He died over a year ago."

Lora looked confused, but Eva could tell that it was dawning on her what this could mean.

"They were sending me a message to *not* visit them," Eva said. "Why would they be sending me a message like that?"

SAM

"You grew up around here?" Sam asked while driving the car. The dawn had broken, bathing the countryside in a warm, yellow glow. After breakfast they'd left the highway, eventually winding their way along quiet country lanes, cutting through dusty farms that hadn't seen rain in a long while.

"Yep," Tobias replied. "Watch the road ahead."

"I'm watching," Sam said, his hands tight on the steering wheel.

"There's a tractor coming."

"I can see."

"Keep steady as it passes."

"I got it."

"Keep to the side of the road, give him room."

"I got it."

Sam did his best to keep the car steady as the big tractor trundled by.

"OK, you're doing good," Tobias said, relaxing a little.

"Told you I could drive," Sam said. "Hey, how come you're letting me drive anyway?"

"Well, you're only a month or so off driving age, and if this race wasn't on, that's what would be ahead for you. Besides, driving is a very useful skill to have. Someone needs to teach you."

"Right. Well, thanks."

"Anytime," Tobias said, chuckling. "Take this next right."

Sam indicated for the turn, slowing down to a near stop as he turned onto a road that soon disintegrated into loose gravel.

"What'd you do for fun out here?" Sam asked, looking over the same endless fields of barren dirt stretching out around them.

"Eyes on the road. Well, when it wasn't baseball season, I'd be building stuff," Tobias said. "Little inventions—I think it's a bit of a Dreamer trait."

"Yeah, I'm not sure if I got much of the creative gene," Sam replied. He eased off the accelerator as they rounded a bend, the rear tires of the powerful sedan sliding out despite his best efforts. "Sorry."

"It's fine," Tobias said, his hand on the dashboard as Sam steadied them on the worn back road. "Driving around here is a specialized skill set at the best of times. The trucks loaded up from the farms tend to tear up the roads. Just take it slow into every turn."

"Doesn't look like the best of times at the moment," Sam said, noting the dry brown grass.

"I haven't been here in about five years," Tobias said,

his eyes taking in the scenery. "It's stuck in a long drought, though. And Duke probably doesn't use the road at all."

"Duke?"

"My uncle." Tobias smiled.

"You have an uncle? Man, he must be *really* old," Sam said, grinning as he drove down the long straight road. The sun was not yet high in the sky and already he could tell that today would be another scorching hot, dry day.

"Yeah, well, he is old, actually. He's my great-uncle," Tobias clarified. "Must be ninety-two or ninety-three now."

"So only a few years older than you then," Sam said, and they laughed.

"OK, take the driveway on your left up here, by the big tree."

Sam slowed the car and took the turn, seeing a large mailbox sitting at the end of a miniature rail track that ran along the length of a long fence.

"Is that mailbox . . ?"

"Yep," Tobias said, grinning. "It's a monorail system, automatically takes itself up to the house after any mail or deliveries arrive."

"You made that?" Sam asked, taking the dirt road towards the house.

"No," Tobias said, shaking his head. Ahead was a large squat wooden house with wraparound verandahs and a couple of huge barns tucked in the paddock behind. "That's Duke's handiwork."

ALEX

"**S**ure you don't want any help?" Phoebe asked.

"Not yet, Mom, thanks," Alex said. He moved over to the table where he'd been working while his mother had slept, finally succumbing to tiredness. Rick had been watching quietly from his post at the door. "You know while you were sleeping before?"

"Yes . . ." Phoebe said.

"Well, prepare yourself—meet Apollo 13, Mark 2!" Alex replied, pulling the sheet off his invention.

"What on earth is *that?*"

"Sure, she ain't pretty," Alex said, looking over his handiwork. "And she sure wouldn't pass NASA testing, but she might just do the job."

"And what might *that* be, exactly?" Phoebe said.

Alex looked at her in mock surprise. "Can't you tell? It's a sub-orbital jet-powered super-elevator, of course."

"Right. Of course." Phoebe now looked at the platform with even less hope. She looked at Rick, who simply shrugged. "Well, sorry, but it looks like something Dr. Frankenstein would put together if he switched from bodies to . . . scrap metal?"

"This here's an oven door," Alex said, rapping his knuckles on the stainless steel panel. "Found that over there," he pointed across the room. "Can't imagine what they were cooking, don't want to know. Now it's our seating platform. The rest are bits and pieces I found around the lab."

"And these?" Phoebe asked, inspecting the four huge hoses, pointing down and secured to the corners of the seating platform.

"Our jet boosters," Alex said.

"Formerly fire hoses?"

"*Industrial* fire hoses—very powerful," Alex replied. "And the water's on, I, ah, checked it earlier." He motioned to where there was a huge puddle around a drain in the corner. The drain was now stuffed with rags to completely block it.

"And you want me to do what, exactly?"

"I want you to trust me," Alex said, breaking into a grin.

"Trust you . . . that this will get us out of here?"

"Just you wait and see," Alex said confidently. "Now hop on. You too, Rick."

Rick came over, inspecting Alex's creation. "Not bad."

Phoebe raised her eyebrows.

"Hey, he breaks our necks, it's your fault—he's your kid," Rick laughed.

"No way! You're going to think I'm a genius!" Alex declared.

"Or," she replied, "we'll forever be stuck down here, drowned, and then we'll never know what your true potential might have been."

"C'mon, Mom, have a little faith!"

The three of them climbed onto the platform, cramming together to fit aboard the makeshift jet-powered elevator Alex had assembled.

"All right . . . ready?" Alex asked as Phoebe fidgeted, trying to get steady and keep her balance next to him. Rick looked like he was barely hanging on by a fingernail. He gave an OK signal with his fingers.

"As ready as I'll ever be . . . you're really serious about trying out this super-sub-elevator-jet thing?" Phoebe said.

"Sub-orbital jet-powered super-elevator. Yep. Saw something similar to it on TV once," Alex said. "They lifted a car into the air with fire hoses."

"Cars don't have bones that can break."

"True, but they *are* a lot heavier," Alex countered. "Hang on, everybody."

He pulled on a rope that was connected to a pulley, which in turn opened four separate valves, each connected to the fire hoses—one in this room, one in the adjoining storeroom, another by the closed blast door, and one behind the lab benches. Alex swallowed hard and his mother hugged him tight, as the three of them watched the hoses fill and stiffen as the water gushed in four almighty torrents. Alex pulled again on the rope, opening the valves further, and soon all four hoses were spewing out water at full capacity.

"Is this all that's meant to be happening?" Phoebe shouted over the deafening rush of water. "That we get drenched?"

"Just make sure you're hanging on tight!" Alex said. "Wait for—"

They began to rise into the air, the platform lifting slowly from the immense water pressure below, like an elevator going up into the large air vent above.

Then they stopped.

They were hovering inside the air vent cavity, about three yards clear of the ground, the tile floor flooding underneath them.

"We're stuck!" Phoebe said. "We're not going any higher!"

"It's OK, we're not stuck," Alex said, carefully adjusting his balance on their seating platform. "That's as high as the force of the water will take us."

"You knew that?"

"I planned on it!" Alex said, watching the water in the room below. There was already a foot or so of water underneath them.

"We're still a long way from the top," Phoebe said, looking at the dot of daylight way above them, where the ventilation shaft brought in air to the underground labyrinth.

"When the room below us is full of water," Alex said, "the water will then fill this shaft."

"And we'll rise like a cork," Phoebe said, finally understanding the entire plan.

"All the way up to the top!" Rick added.

"And out of here!" Alex said. "The Archimedes displacement principle at work."

His mother looked shocked and said, "Archimedes?"

"Only one of our greatest-ever Dreamers. Don't you know your Dreamer history?" Alex grinned.

"Will you ever stop surprising me?" Phoebe leaned over to hug him again and the shift of weight on their little platform threatened to topple them all.

"Mom!" Alex said, leaning away to counterbalance her. "Save the hugs until we're out of here."

SAM

"**M**aybe no one's home," Sam said, watching as Tobias knocked on the door again and then peered through the window. There was no sound coming from inside the house, only the birds chirping and fluttering past the verandah in the morning sun.

"He'll be around," Tobias replied. "Let's check the barns."

They walked together from the creaky old verandah to the largest of the two barns. Sam could see its smaller neighbor was open at one end and full of the kind of equipment you'd expect to see on a working farm. This big barn, however, was far, far different.

"Maybe cover your ears," Tobias warned.

Sam followed his advice, and Tobias pressed a large red button under a sign that read:

RING AT OWN PERIL

This was no ordinary doorbell—it was more like an alarm and the sound rang out so loudly that it rattled Sam's bones. Dozens of birds shot up from the surrounding fields and flapped away in fright.

"That was crazy loud!" Sam said.

"Yep," Tobias said, wincing from the sound that still rang in their ears. "Duke is more than a little deaf."

There was a jiggling sound on the other side of the solid barn door and then it opened, revealing a stooped man with bright, searching eyes.

"As I live and breathe—Tobias!" Duke exclaimed, standing at the big barn doors and pulling Tobias into a backslapping hug. "How have you been, son?"

"I'm good!" Tobias shouted in reply. "And you look well!"

"Never better," Duke said, slapping his flat stomach under his overalls and grinning with shiny white dentures. "And who's this whippersnapper you've got with you?"

"This is my friend Sam."

Sam shook Duke's outstretched hand, the strong and rough handshake of someone who had spent a lifetime working with tools.

"Please, come to the house, I'll put the kettle on," Duke said, pointing to the old farmhouse.

"That sounds wonderful," Tobias yelled, before adding, "Duke, do you mind if we leave something in the barn first? Just for safekeeping while we're here?"

"Safest place on the ranch," Duke said, still smiling. "I can never find anything in there!"

Tobias chuckled, and Sam looked at him, confused.

"The Gears," Tobias explained, soft enough that Sam knew Duke wouldn't have a chance of overhearing. "In case we have any unwanted visitors. The barn will be the best place to hide them while we're here."

Sam nodded, looking over Tobias' shoulder into the mammoth barn. Beyond an empty area near the doors, he could see mountains of machinery and equipment overshadowing a long work bench that stood to one side. It was littered with metal off-cuts, gadgets and all kinds of hand tools. Towers of hay bales were stacked floor-to-ceiling all around the walls.

While Tobias chatted and reminisced with Duke, Sam went inside and concealed the Gears in a low corner of the dim barn, between two bales of hay, behind a stack of rusty pitchforks.

"OK, I'm done," Sam said, coming out and shutting the barn door behind him.

They headed across the paddock to the old house. Flocks of birds now dotted the wide-open skies and there were rabbits and other little creatures moving through the grass. There was peace here—peace and solitude the likes of which Sam couldn't remember.

Tobias and Duke talked as they walked together, catching up on years of small, and loud, talk.

"Ah, that's better," Duke said, putting his hearing aids in. "Make sure you boys have some of that fruitcake, made it myself, old family recipe."

"It's delicious," Sam said, finding the cake almost too hard to bite through.

"What's that, sonny?"

"It's delicious!" Sam repeated, louder.

"What is?" Duke said.

"This cake," Sam said, hiding the rest in his napkin and sipping his tea.

"Oh, don't eat that," Duke said. "Been lying around for ages. Haven't baked in years. Now, where'd I put my hearing aids . . ."

"They're in, Duke," Tobias said.

"Ah yes, so they are. Need to turn them up is all," he said. "Now, my glasses. Has anyone seen my glasses?"

"Ah, they're on top of your head," Sam said. He looked to Tobias in concern.

And this guy's going to help us, how?

"And so they are! Thank you, Dan."

"Sam."

"Pardon?"

Sam looked to Tobias.

"Duke," Tobias said, sitting forward and close to his uncle. "Is my room still as I left it?"

"Yes, of course." Duke's face broke into a big smile. His lips, eyes, all of his face full of creases and lines. "Why would I change it?"

"Well, it's been a while," Tobias said.

"I knew you'd be home from college sooner or later,"

Duke said, getting up and walking slowly over to the kitchen counter. "I'm going to put some more tea on. Think I have some left—not much, mind, what with the war rations and all."

Tobias stood and Sam followed suit.

"What war?" Sam asked Tobias. "Does he—does he think we're at war here?"

"You make the tea!" Tobias said. "I'll show my friend Sam my room!"

"The broom?" Duke said. "In the laundry!"

Sam followed Tobias up rickety stairs, which had a chair on an electric rail to one side.

"Despite what your first impressions may be," Tobias said, "Duke is still the brightest mind I've ever known."

"I don't doubt it," Sam said. "My mom used to get like that and she's about half his age."

"That reminds me," Tobias said, pausing at a closed door at the end of the long hall. "We'll speak with the director about your parents, see if we can contact them."

Sam nodded.

"If you still want to?"

"I . . . yeah, I do." Sam thought about the parents who raised him—a loving family that turned out not to be a family at all. "But there's so much going on," Sam added, "so, I mean, there's no rush . . ."

Tobias nodded, still paused in the hallway. He smiled then opened the door. "In the meantime, you ain't seen nothing like this."

10

EVA

"You know," Lora said, panting for breath. "There's such a thing as *over*training."

"I want to be ready to defend myself," Eva said, getting into another jujitsu fighting stance. "Let's go!"

"You're ready," Lora said, settling herself. "Trust me, you're a natural at this, and you'll be able to defend yourself. What you've shown in the past twenty-four hours is better than most of the sixth-year students back at the Academy."

"In every generation there is a Chosen One," Eva said in a mock voice-over tone. "She alone will stand against the vampires, the demons and the mean girls at school."

"You've seen too many teen movies, I think." Lora laughed.

"I'm using my generation's heroes to inspire me, that's all," Eva said. "Come on, let's spar again."

"You're fine, training is over for the day, young slayer."

"Still, I could get better," Eva said, dancing around on the spot, eyes on Lora. "I'm ready!"

Lora laughed. "And I'm beat," she said, sitting down on the sofa in their hotel room, which had been pushed against the walls like most of the other furniture to create the makeshift dojo.

"Fine, leave me defenseless," Eva said, taking a seat next to Lora—who pounced up and went to get her in a headlock. Eva was prepared and moved her body with her opponent's to flip Lora on her back.

"Argh, OK, OK!" Lora said, laughing. "You're some kind of hyper-evolved ninja in the guise of a sixteen-year-old girl. I give up. You are now the master."

Eva laughed too and helped her teacher up to her feet. "I should totally have my own theme music."

"Meanwhile, back in the real world," Lora said, "we have to get to the airport."

Eva jumped up to her feet and motioned that she was ready.

They took two bottles of water from the minibar fridge and left their room, walking down the corridor to the elevator lobby. Lora pressed the down button.

"So," Eva said, "think Mac's guys are still back in Vancouver looking for us?"

"With any luck," Lora replied, "they're still running around in circles."

"Who are they?"

"My guess would be mercenaries—guys who used to be soldiers but now work for the highest bidder, no matter who they are and what they're up to. They're highly trained, so we don't want to get caught by them."

"What would they do?"

"They'd take us in."

"Ha, then Mac would just have to arrange a way for us to 'escape' again."

"Mmmm, maybe," Lora mused.

"You sound like you don't believe Mac," Eva said.

"I don't *trust* Mac," Lora corrected. "Where *is* this elevator?" She pressed the down button again twice, then went to check her holstered dart pistol before recalling that it was no longer there.

"So why did he let us go then? And what about my aunt?" Eva asked, confused, and worried now.

"The more I think about the last few days, the more I believe that the whole thing was an elaborate show, for us and the Academy, to gain our trust. As useful as you might be to him later in the race, I think Mac's hoping that releasing us will make it easier for him to get his hands on who he really wants—Sam. Your aunt probably truly believes he is on our side."

"But really, he'd tell lies about anything?" Eva asked.

"Yes, I think so."

They turned to the elevator as it finally pinged its arrival. The doors opened and four of Mac's men stood there, looking straight at them.

11

ALEX

"OK, see you then," Phoebe said, ending her call to the director.

They were in the emergency department at Vancouver General Hospital, waiting to have Alex's arm checked out.

Alex's invention had worked. The lab had filled with water, pushing them up into the ventilation tower. Once they reached the surface, they had run to the cover of the dense woodland surrounding the perimeter of the complex. Alex had wanted to go back inside the building to look for the other Agents, but Phoebe had insisted they follow Enterprise protocol and retreat to safety immediately while Rick checked up on the rest of the team.

"We're meeting Jack in Washington, DC, tonight," she said to Alex.

"What's in Washington, DC?" Alex asked.

"He wouldn't say over the phone, but I think it's to do with Stella."

"Figures," Alex said. "Hey, Mom, do you think, if it came to it, you could take out Stella?"

Phoebe laughed. "Sure," she said. "If it came to a fight, I'd take her down."

"Really?"

"You don't think I could?"

They both laughed, and a nurse came over and explained that they would be seen in the next hour after a few more-urgent cases waiting in the emergency room.

"Any word from Sam?" Alex asked.

Phoebe looked a little worried, but then said, "He's with Tobias, headed for the next Gear."

"Oh, man . . ."

"What?"

Alex shrugged, remained silent.

Eventually, Phoebe said, "Do you want anything to eat or drink?"

"Nah, I'm OK."

They sat in the waiting room, watching the other patients and the busy medical staff.

"You'll get your chance," Phoebe said after a few minutes.

"Yeah, I know. Not much good now anyway, with this mortal injury." He held up his arm.

"You'll have to be patient, Alex."

"But I haven't had any dreams yet, you know, none about the Gears, or Solaris."

"That's a good thing," Phoebe said. "You'll have that dream when you're meant to. And just think, when you do—"

"I'll be ready, yeah, I know." Alex thought about the possibilities of what might be ahead. *Imagine being the first one to cross the finish line . . . I'll be a hero. Cool . . .*

"You're letting me go on an undercover mission?" Alex couldn't believe his luck.

I'm so getting my own dart gun this time!

In a private viewing room in the Smithsonian, the director, along with Phoebe, Alex and three Agents, sat and watched a briefing on a large wall screen. The Professor and Jedi were also linked via video conference from the Academy, as was Shiva from the Enterprise base in Amsterdam.

They all were studying the schematics of the Washington Monument, which were displayed on the screen.

"You can see that the foundation system goes a long way underground," Shiva said over the line, controlling the image remotely. "There, it taps into the electromagnetic power field via a Tesla device."

"You're sure about this?" Phoebe asked.

"It's true," the Professor said from his office. "The Washington Monument was opened a few years before the Eiffel Tower and serves the same purpose."

"To record dream waves?" Alex asked.

"That's right," the director said. "The technology was

nicknamed 'Dream Sweeper' and used Tesla's original machines that he invented while researching wireless energy—"

"When he rediscovered the Dreamscape," Alex interjected. "Sorry for butting in," he apologized to the director.

"That's fine—I'm glad you know your history. And yes, that's true too. And," the director said, "this was all happening back when governments thought they could use the information they gathered from people's dreams."

"With the help of some members from the earlier Dreamer Councils," the Professor added. "Part of our history that I'm not proud of."

"This technology has provided a huge amount of scientific data for those of us in the Dreamer community to analyze," the director reasoned.

"I know," the Professor said. "But without the knowledge, or more importantly, consent, of those whose dreams were recorded."

"So what's the current status of the Washington Monument?" Phoebe asked, getting them back to the mission at hand.

"It was mothballed," the director said, studying the schematic. "No longer active, like that ex-Enterprise site in Vancouver you were caught up in."

Alex knew that something wasn't being said. "That site and this are connected?" he asked.

"Yes," the director said slowly. "You know that we were looking for a code book at the Vancouver complex?"

"Yes," Alex said. "Too bad there wasn't a Gear there."

"That would have been a lucky bonus, very lucky. No, the team's primary instructions were to retrieve a code book we believe was still held in the vault there. The book contains all the unique codes to unlock and activate sites such as the one at the Washington Monument. Unfortunately we were too late."

"And whoever has that," the Professor said, "now—"

"Stella has it!" Alex said. "I mean, she has to. Her Agents were down in those labs."

"We know Mac was there too," the director said.

"And since we know Stella hasn't left the continental US yet, our best bet is that she's headed straight for the closest tower—the Washington Monument."

"Either way," the Professor said, "someone else now has control over Dream Sweeper sites across the world, giving them the ability to record every detail of every dream within the radius of the tower. They'll have access to all that information—and they'll have the locations of all those who dream."

"They'll find us!" Alex said.

"Not if we head off whoever has that code book," the director said. "Then we can stop them."

Alex stood up. "When do we leave?"

12

"This was your bedroom growing up?" Sam asked, looking around the room lit by the dim light peeking through the closed curtains. It was crammed full of all kinds of toys, gadgets and inventions, mostly handmade metal trains, cars and remote airplanes. Wires, wheels, nuts and bolts, a million pieces of metal and wood and plastic littered every surface and most of the floor.

"Until high school, yeah, this was it," Tobias said, pulling back the curtains to open the windows, flooding the room with light and air. "Then I went to the Academy and boarded at around your age. But this was home for me—always was, always will be."

"It's awesome!" Sam looked around. There was a steam-powered catapult, a model volcano Sam thought looked like it was still bubbling quietly in the corner and a miniature hot air balloon hanging from the ceiling. The shelves were stuffed with figurines and windup robots made from reclaimed body parts of action figures. Skyscraper-like towers of well-thumbed comic books stood on either side of the overflowing bookshelves, alongside a couple of buckets of battered baseballs.

"Looks like Santa's workshop in here," Sam said in awe.

"Didn't you know?" Tobias said, "I am Santa Claus!"

"Ha!" Sam said, rolling his eyes. He picked up a pair of homemade night-vision goggles mounted to an old bicycle helmet.

"It's dusty in here," Tobias said, running a finger along a shelf, bent under the weight of all the books. "I really should visit Duke more often, help out around here."

"I reckon he's invented all the help he needs with all his gadgets," Sam said. "What are we looking for again?"

"This!" Tobias said, taking a helmet off an old table.

"And that is . . ?"

"My Home Video Magnificent Mind Machine," Tobias said, looking nostalgically over the contraption. "Or HVMMM. Never was much good at naming my inventions."

"Huh?" Sam asked, looking at the bizarre helmet. Next to it on the table sat a large black box.

"It's a prototype dream recorder," Tobias said. "It paved the way for what I designed with Jedi back at the Academy. Have a look while I figure out what to do about rewiring the power adapter."

Sam took the helmet, surprised at how heavy it was in his hands. "I think this will break my neck."

"Yeah, probably best to wear it while lying down," Tobias said, getting out a tool kit and going to work on the power pack.

"Well, if the Academy's current version—"

"The Mark 7," Tobias interrupted.

"The Mark 7, right," Sam said, sitting on a chair with the helmet on his lap. "So if the Academy's one is a modern-day hybrid car, this thing would be a horse and cart from the Middle Ages? Is that about right?"

"Fair analogy. Although unlike the cart, this is one of a kind. Aha!"

Tobias found some new-looking batteries and inserted them—but they were long dead.

"'Use by 1989,'" Sam read from the back of the package. "Hmm, spring-clean much?"

Tobias laughed. "I was never much good at throwing things out . . . 1989, that was a good year."

"If you say so . . ." Sam rolled his eyes, then joined in searching the room. It was stocked floor-to-ceiling like a museum of Tobias' early life, but no more batteries were discovered.

"Come on, we'll see if Duke has got some. If not, we'll go into town."

"Hey, what does this do?" Sam asked, reaching out to a tiny lever that said DO NOT TOUCH! It was connected to a toy train track that ran up the wall, along the ceiling and through a hole in the wall.

"Hmm, you know, I can't quite remember," Tobias said, scratching his chin. "Try it."

Sam hesitated for just a second, then flicked the lever.

Nothing happened.

"Oh yes," Tobias said, opening the window and turning on a little fan that was clipped on to the window frame. A wire ran from the fan to a tiny generator, which hummed to life and glowed red. "Try again."

Sam toggled the lever on and off a few times until a radio cranked into life somewhere underneath a pile of comic books. Then the lights in the ceiling flickered.

CLONK!

A yellow toy train engine came to life and emerged from behind a line of books, its headlamp shining brightly.

"Ha!" Tobias said, his eyes sparkling.

Sam watched the train travel through a tunnel, which in turn switched on a television. The train continued down a slope and exited the room through the hole in the wall.

"Where does it go?" Sam asked, peering into the hole. It was too dark to see anything.

"It used to go through the walls and floor, downstairs to the kitchen pantry, and raid the chocolate supply," Tobias said. "Though I doubt that Duke has the kitchen stocked like he used to."

Sam nodded. The television showed grainy footage of the train as it traveled along the track, relayed from a camera built into the front engine.

"Did you have parents?" Sam asked. "Real ones—I mean, you know . . ."

"Did I ever know my real parents?" Tobias clarified for him.

Sam nodded.

"Yes, but they—"

"Arghhh!" Duke's shout rattled through the old wooden house from downstairs.

Tobias sprinted from the room, hurdling obstacles in the way, Sam close behind.

They found Duke in the kitchen, hunched over the sink. To one side of the kitchen counter, Sam saw that the little train had derailed after leaving the pantry and crashed against the kettle.

"Sorry, Duke!" Tobias shouted, going to his aid. "I should have warned you before sending that down here."

Sam saw that Duke's face was damp with sweat and it looked as though he was having a heart attack.

"I think he's in trouble," Tobias said, concerned. Then he spoke loudly to Duke, "I'll help you to your chair!"

"Wait!" Sam swallowed hard. In the window above the sink, Sam could see a small hole in the glass. Tracking the line of the hole to Duke, now completely unconscious, he saw a tiny dart in the old man's chest. He pointed at it.

Tobias stared at it wide-eyed.

They had visitors.

13

EVA

Time stood still for a split second as Eva weighed up the odds—four huge guys in front of her, Lora next to her.

Attack is the best form of defense . . .

Lora moved first.

Eva was right behind her.

They rushed towards the elevator, their sudden attack momentarily catching the men off guard. In the confined space, the four huge guys couldn't use the advantage of their bulk. Lora and Eva used speed and surprise.

Eva hit the closest guy as he was drawing his dart pistol, and before it clattered to the floor of the elevator she'd smashed him in the solar plexus, doubling him over.

The next guy wasn't so easy. Eva ducked under the swing of his arm—which then connected to the head of one of his comrades. Lora demolished one attacker and then flipped another around.

Eva used the moment of confusion between the two hulking men to attack again—she took one guy's arm and twisted it behind his head into a compliance hold. He wriggled and resisted.

He's too strong, he's going to break out of my hold—

Eva let go as she felt his weight drop.

She looked down at the four men on the floor of the elevator lobby, stun darts embedded in their backs. Lora stood over their unconscious bodies, holding the dart pistol.

"That was amazing!" Eva said, catching her breath.

"I only took out the guy to the right," Lora said. "You took down those three—looks like all that practice paid off."

"I don't even know how, or what just happened . . ." Eva said, relaxing from her jujitsu stance and looking at her fists in awe. "I just kind of—flipped a switch. Who knew I could do that?"

"I've created a monster," Lora said, a hint of pride in her voice. She was then serious again as she scanned the hallways. "These guys won't be alone. We're going to have to get out of here—right now."

They took the fire escape, racing down the metal stairs at the rear of the hotel. A few floors from the ground, Eva could make out cop cars parked at each end of the alley.

"Would they be working for Mac?" Eva asked.

"Probably," Lora said. "He has connections everywhere."

"How do we get out of here?"

"This way," Lora said, slipping down the remaining stairs and jumping from the last landing into the hotel's loading bay, where several vans were parked. "We'll stow away."

"Wait," Eva said, taking one last peek around at the cops. They were stopping all the vehicles exiting.

Shoot.

"No, we can't get out that way."

"OK, plan B," Lora said, and her Stealth Suit changed into a Seattle PD uniform. Eva copied it flawlessly.

"Think we pass as cops?" Eva asked, nervous.

"I think I do," Lora said. "But your hair is probably non-regulation."

Eva caught the reflection of her spiky black hair and thick dark eyeliner in the rear window of a van.

"Give me a sec," Eva said, turning to a dripping faucet behind them and turning it on. She pulled her hand across her face and smoothed down her hair. A minute later there was no trace of makeup and her hair was slicked back neatly and tucked under her police cap.

"That'll do it," Lora said. "OK, let's take the alley."

"And what, walk right past the cop cars?" Eva asked as she fell into step next to Lora. They were approaching the southern end of the alley.

"No, not quite," Lora said, taking her dart gun out of its holster and adjusting the amount of sedative that each projectile would contain. "Just follow my lead."

Lora approached two police officers, who turned their way after clearing a delivery van to pass through. She smiled.

"Howdy, officers," the first one said, his hands resting on his hips. "Nice day."

"You have no idea," Lora replied, taking a quick look up and down the alley to make sure that there were no onlookers. She swiftly pulled the dart gun from behind her back and dropped them both with a shot to the legs before they could blink. "Quick, help me put them in the doorway so they can't be seen," she murmured to Eva, who stood and stared in shock.

As they shifted the first unconscious cop, his police uniform changed before their eyes into the standard dull metal-gray of a Stealth Suit.

"Well," Lora said, leaving him on the side of the street. "Now I don't feel so bad about darting them. We'll leave them here."

"Who are they?" Eva asked, looking at the other guy with the dart in his leg, his Stealth Suit now also visible.

"I'm betting they're reinforcements for those guys upstairs, so they're probably here on Mac's orders," Lora replied, getting into the high-performance cop car and revving the engine as Eva got in the passenger seat. She dropped the car into gear and expertly made the tight turn away from the alley, tires squealing in protest at the speed. "And we're not going to hang around to find out if I'm right."

14

No sooner had Sam and Tobias registered the dart in Duke's chest, than the front door was blasted off its hinges and sent flying across the room. Agents rushed into the kitchen, weapons drawn. Sam could hear windows shattering as more enemies entered the house through every vantage point.

"Don't move!" a commanding voice rang out.

Sam and Tobias froze. Together they stood under the watchful gaze of the armed men.

"Place your hands on top of your head," one of the Agents ordered, moving slowly to Tobias and binding his wrists with strong plastic ties. Then he leveled the dart gun at Sam's neck.

"You didn't need to dart Duke," Tobias protested. "He's too old to be treated like that."

The leader of the group said nothing. There were seven of them now, all alert, ready to shoot given the opportunity.

Sam struggled against the guy who was putting ties on his wrists behind his back.

"Where are you taking us?" Sam asked the leader.

No answer.

They were led to the couch and pushed down to sit uncomfortably, their hands tied tightly. Sam immediately thought of the Gears hidden in the barn and was relieved that he had taken them out of his backpack that still sat in the corner of the room.

"We'll never tell you anything," Sam said, defiant.

Still the men said nothing, although the leader had two guys put Duke on the other sofa, where he snored like an old steam train.

"Don't bother with them," Tobias said to Sam. "They're just the muscle. They've clearly been watching this place, waiting for the moment we got here."

Sam understood what he meant. These Agents had undoubtedly been monitoring the house, waiting to see if Tobias, and possibly Sam, would show up. They would report in their catch and await new orders.

"We walked into a trap," Sam said to Tobias. "What do we do now?"

"We wait . . ."

"I thought we'd be seeing you soon," Tobias said to Stella as she strode towards them. "This op had all the hallmarks of your ruthlessness."

It had taken no more than an hour for a jet to arrive,

landing almost silently in the paddock outside. Sam could see it touch down through the open doors of the barn, so much like the Academy's jet—able to fly undetected and to land vertically like a helicopter.

Stella stood in front of them. They had been moved to the main barn and strapped to chairs in the vast space. The Agents were now out of sight. Sam had been running through scenarios in his mind for the last hour, how Tobias and he could somehow overwhelm them—but it seemed impossible.

"I don't have much use for you, Tobias," Stella said acidly, "so I'd keep your tone pleasant if I were you."

"And me?" Sam asked. "You have use for me, right?"

"Oh, like you wouldn't *believe*," Stella said through a sneer. She bent down to open a rugged black case on the barn floor before them.

Inside the case, Sam could see a notebook computer, hooked up to a dream recorder. She was planning to enter his subconscious mind and draw out every little detail from his dreams.

She's not getting anything from me.

"I know that you're familiar with these," Stella said to Sam as she powered the machine up. "We're going to watch the playback of your most recent dream—don't bother talking."

"Good luck with that," Sam said.

Focus, Sam. Gotta hold out—gotta shut her out of your mind.

"The benefit of no longer having a boss, or any rules," Stella said, "is that I can set any limit on these controls that I wish."

Sam strained against his straps.

"Careful," Stella said, walking over and placing two postage stamp-sized electrodes on his temples. "The more you struggle, and the more you try to hide your dream, the more I will have to ramp up the power. You don't want to try resisting a dream recorder—it can leave you, shall we say, a little less smart in waking life."

Sam looked to Tobias.

"Oh, he hasn't warned you?" Stella said, smiling. "Interesting . . ."

"What's she mean, *less smart?*" Sam asked Tobias.

"Oh, go on, Tobias," Stella goaded, "why don't you tell your little friend here what can happen if he fights the machine on dream recall."

Sam swallowed hard, felt sweat beading on his forehead.

"It has dangers, if you fight it," Tobias said quietly to Sam. "They are delving so deep into the core of your memory that if you resist it can cause permanent memory issues."

"What kind of issues?" Sam said.

"Worst case? Amnesia."

Sam gulped.

OK, new plan. Let them have this one. We'll all see where the dream leads . . . we'll just have to beat them to it.

He nodded to Tobias that he understood what had to be done.

"OK," Sam said to Stella, trying to sound indifferent. "Go ahead."

The dream machine was like the others at the Academy, with a few small differences—this seemed more advanced, and Stella gave him an accompanying sedative through a dart gun, jabbing him in the arm with it like a bad-tempered nurse with a sharp needle.

Sam blinked twice, then was out.

As the waves of unconsciousness dragged him under, he was aware that this time he was not driving things as he'd been learning how to do. The dream world appeared around him, memories of the same desert canyons from before, but as he watched, detached, his dream went into rewind, going into a prelude that he hadn't recalled before.

He saw a road sign:

15

EVA

"Still no answer from Tobias," Eva said, ending the call.

"It's not like him to miss a scheduled check-in," Lora said, driving on a freeway, Seattle's outer suburbs disappearing fast behind them. "Call Jedi, have him try to track their phone."

"OK," Eva said, calling the Academy and putting it on speakerphone.

"Yo, this is Jedi."

"Jedi, it's Eva and Lora here," Eva said.

"Hey, girl power!" Jedi replied, his voice suddenly animated. "How goes it in the field? Hope you're leaving some bad guys for the others to sort out."

Eva relayed what had happened back at the hotel.

"So you're in a *police* vehicle now?" Jedi said.

"Yep," Lora replied.

"I'd ditch it if I were you," Jedi said. "They might be able to track it. And it's not very inconspicuous. Rent a car or something."

"As soon as we can," Lora agreed, pulling off the main road onto an exit ramp. "Jedi, I need you to track Tobias."

"Already have. I know where he is," Jedi said. "He's at his old place outside Amarillo."

Eva asked, "Can you contact him?"

"Hang on, I'll try now," Jedi said. They heard the phone ringing out. "Hmm, no answer. Let's switch to vision . . ."

They waited a moment, and could hear Jedi's fingers tapping away at his keyboards.

"Jedi?" Eva said, when it had been quiet for a while.

"Ah, yeah, I'm here," he said, distracted. "OK, look, I've managed to hack into a military satellite to look at the area . . . scanning now."

"What do you see?" Lora asked.

"Looks like their party got crashed," Jedi said. "We've got several large SUV vehicles surrounding the farmhouse and—oh boy, we've got a jet landed there too. One of the missing stealth aircraft from the Enterprise."

"Stella," Lora said.

"Yep," Jedi replied. "Though I'm not getting any register of people on scene via thermal imaging, except two in the barn and one in the house. And none of them are moving."

"They're hostages," Lora said, parking the cop car in the parking lot of a shopping mall. "And Stella's probably there with a team. The latest gen Suits don't show up on thermal cameras."

"I reckon that's about the size of it—the satellite can't track them," Jedi replied.

"OK, keep your eyes on the farm," Lora said. "Alert

everyone anywhere near the area to head there to set up a rescue mission. Don't let Sam and Tobias out of your sight. We'll head there now."

"Got it," Jedi replied.

"And call us if anything develops," Lora said.

"Right. Good luck." Jedi signed off.

Lora opened her car door. "Come on, Eva," she said. "We're ditching this car and getting something a little faster."

"Faster?" Eva said, following Lora's lead. "What's faster than a cop car?"

Lora pointed. "That."

16

SAM'S NIGHTMARE

I pull over in Tobias' car. There's a gas station and a diner, and a collection of converted sheds in a long row, each offering different services to tourists. My feet scrunch on the gravel, and I do a double take at one of the billboard signs—CODY'S ADVENTURE TOURS.

I walk in through the door of the office. There is no one inside.

I call out, "Hello?"

I go around to the back—that's empty too. There's just another office and a small adjoining storage room. I head out to the parking lot, walking slowly around the building. There's a huge shed with a big roller door that is open. It's dark inside but as I approach I can see, in the light of the skylight panels, a familiar face.

Cody.

"Hi!" I call, walking towards him.

"Hey," Cody says, strapping down adventure touring equipment—what looks like a yacht's sail. "Today's tours don't start until this afternoon."

"That's OK," I say, looking around. 'I'm here about something else . . ."

Everything shudders and freezes around me, like a TV replay skipping frames and pausing. The world spins to a new scene, shudders again and unfreezes.

I am in a kayak. The water is calm—so far. Ahead it's another story.

"Cody?"

"Here," Cody says, paddling to catch up. "You're a natural at this—nearly lost you, it's like you jumped ahead at the speed of light."

"Yeah, well, guns like these," I say, flexing my non-existent biceps, "you know how it is."

Cody chuckles.

I look forward to where the water is white and foamy, swirling around rapidly. There are steep canyon walls on either side. As the passage between the cliffs ahead narrows, the water pulls us forward at a quickening rate.

"Cody? How do we . . ." I pause and look beside me. Cody's kayak drifts by, empty. "Cody? Cody!"

I can't see him anywhere. I stand up in the kayak and dive into the cold water.

I must find him . . .

SAM

"Sam!"

Sam opened his eyes. Details of Duke's barn slowly came into focus. Tobias was still tied to the seat opposite, struggling against his straps. The dream recording device was on the barn floor, just as it had been before. Sam could feel the little electrodes still stuck to his temples.

So am I really awake? Or is this just another jump in my dream?

"Sam—now's our chance!" Tobias said, crookedly standing up, still tied to the chair, and then sitting down again, hard. The rickety old wooden chair creaked loudly under him. Sam watched, still in a daze, as Tobias repeated this two more times before the chair splintered apart completely—Tobias was free. He rushed to Sam. "Stella's gone, come on, quick."

OK, so this is real, then.

Sam saw that a rogue Agent was crumpled on the floor next to Tobias' chair. "But . . . how?"

"Used my head," Tobias said, rubbing his forehead. "Literally. I pretended to be asleep, and when he came over to check, I head-butted him."

"Awesome," Sam said, getting up as Tobias undid his binds, still a little unsteady on his feet. "How long was I out?"

"About an hour," Tobias replied. "Stella won't be gone

for long, let's go."

"Wait," Sam said, picking up the dream recorder off the floor. He held it high above his head and then threw it down onto the ground. He took the Agent's water bottle and poured water over the broken black box, watching it spark. He ducked into recesses of the barn and retrieved the hidden Gears, securing them safely underneath his Stealth Suit.

"Did you see exactly where the next Dreamer is located?" Tobias asked.

"Yes, but—"

"Nice move, let's go get Duke and get out of here," Tobias said.

"But they'll see us coming!" Sam protested.

Tobias turned and smiled. "This place has a few hidden surprises yet."

"I can't see them . . ." Sam said drowsily. He was crouched alongside Tobias, hidden behind a huge green combine harvester that stood in the paddock close to the barn. The long dry grass came up past Sam's waist and swayed in the afternoon breeze.

"They'll be out there," Tobias said, eyes searching and then looking back towards the farmhouse. "They've boxed in our car."

Sam could see three huge SUVs parked around their car. There was also the huge stealth aircraft in the adjacent paddock on the other side of the house.

Great, that thing is not going to make our getaway any easier. Unless . . .

Sam looked around, trying to spot any Agents patrolling outside the house.

Tobias was silent for a moment and then said, "We can do this another way."

"There's Stella!" Sam pointed. Through the kitchen window, they could see several Agents, including Stella, all sitting down at the table. One Agent stood and went to the window, parting the curtain to look out.

Sam looked down at his Stealth Suit—as long as they stayed relatively still, they were well concealed, the Suits allowing them to blend into their immediate background. Sam winced as a sudden flash from his dream replayed through his mind. He shook his head to try to clear the drowsiness of the sedative that still made it difficult to concentrate on reality.

"Sam . . ?"

"Yeah?" Sam said.

Tobias gave him a nudge, making Sam lose his balance slightly.

"Hey!" Sam protested.

"Just making sure you're alert," Tobias said.

"I am."

"Good. Now, I have a plan, and you have to follow it, no matter what, OK?"

Sam nodded.

Tobias' plan involved returning to the barn and locating a small hatch in the floor, hidden under a pile of hay bales. The hatch opened to reveal a small tunnel that connected the barn to the house.

"I dug this out one year during the summer, when I came home from the Academy," Tobias explained. "Took me weeks. I was planning to run another train system through here, if I remember correctly."

Sam shuddered to think of the spiders that had since made that tunnel their home.

"OK, remember the plan?" Tobias asked Sam as he lowered himself through the hatch door. "Your job is to create a distraction, and then escape. Go as soon as you get the signal from me in the house."

Sam nodded, as Tobias disappeared down into the black tunnel. "Wait! What's the signal?" he whispered loudly into the tunnel after him.

"You'll know when you see it and hear it," came a distant reply from underground.

So, this distraction . . .

Crouching as he made his way through the long grass, Sam climbed up into the seat of the tractor. Parked in front of the harvester, it was huge in its own right. Four wheels at the back, two at the front, with an engine strong enough to tow a few trucks. Coupled to the harvester, it was perfect for the job at hand—to be a wrecking ball.

Sam went through the directions given by Tobias—the key was turned to the ON position, all he had to do was give it one more turn to the next notch which would start the motor. Then he could release the brakes, put it into gear and his foot on the gas would do the rest.

Well, I do have to steer this thing . . .

Sam looked at the water tower close to the house.

Right, wrecking ball.

He closed the glass door to the cabin, staying low down in the chair and as still as possible. He could hear his own accelerated breathing. He watched the house, the silhouettes of Agents through the curtains making themselves at home.

What are they waiting for? They must have thought recording my dreams will take hours by the looks of how relaxed they are.

Sam looked from the house to the aircraft. Sleek and black, and so out of place in this idyllic farm setting.

Plan B.

Sam quickly looked back to the house. Still the same.

Poor old Duke would still be unconscious. Such a small and frail old man, he might be out for days if they'd used the standard amount of tranquilizer in the dart.

Sam imagined Tobias, crawling underground towards the house through the spider-filled tunnel. He shuddered. Then his mind raced through Plan B. Not that he wanted to have to enact it, but it needed to be thought through, just in case.

As Tobias had explained it, Plan B was to be put into motion at the moment that Sam felt he had a chance to escape but Tobias didn't.

The other barn.

Sam could see it. The driveway led to it, skirting around the house as though it formed a roundabout. There was something in there that Tobias called *Bullitt*, and he assured Sam that it would get him out of harm's way if he needed it.

Sam shook off the thought. Plan A would work. It had to. He didn't want to be separated from Tobias, and he didn't want to leave Duke behind with Stella and her gang of—

KLAP-BOOM!

Flames erupted from the kitchen windows of the house. Two rogue Agents flew through the windows, landing in the field.

Nice! That'd be my signal!

Sam turned the key on the tractor. Nothing happened.

He turned the key again. Nothing. Only the control panel lit up. He heard commotion coming from inside the house.

Sam frantically searched the instrument panel before him.

What am I missing?

A fire was raging in the house. The whole side wall where the kitchen had been was now engulfed in flames.

Get out of there, Tobias!

PLINK!

Sam focused on the glass in front of him. Something had hit it.

PLINK!

Darts! Agents were firing at him from on top of the water tower, hitting the front panel of the windshield in quick succession. The glass was thick, built to withstand farming accidents, maybe even tornadoes.

Gotta get moving—how do I start this thing?!

In front of Sam, a big round green glowing button read: START.

Are you kidding me?

Sam pushed the button.

VROOOM!

The tractor was already in gear with the brake off. He pushed his foot down on the gas pedal and the result was instant forward momentum.

VROOOOOM!

"Yeeeeehaaaaaaaa!" Sam called out. "Hang on, Tobias, I'm coming!"

18

As he approached the house and the water tower, his heart raced even faster at the sight of the fire, flames licking up and consuming one side of the wooden house. Agents spilled out of the windows and doors, covering their eyes and mouths from the searing heat and smoke. Sparks flew out of windows as part of the ceiling gave way.

PLINK! PLINK!

Sam turned the wheel of the tractor at the last moment, so that one of the massive rear tires hit the closest leg of the water tower.

The result was instant—and spectacular. The water tower fell like a house of cards towards the farmhouse. Steam erupted and hissed on impact.

Sam turned and looked out of the rear window of the tractor's cab. Behind him he could see that the fallen water tower had sandwiched the trailing harvester against what was left of the back of the house.

Time to get out of here.

Around the other side of the house, Sam could see a couple of Agents out cold on the ground. The sleek black jet reflected the bright-orange flames that were still raging on one side of the house. Water flooded all over as it spilled and sloshed from the toppled tower and over the wooden frame of the farmhouse.

There was movement at the front door—

Tobias was carrying Duke over his shoulder in a fireman's carry, shooting a dart pistol with his other hand as he ran towards the jet.

Tobias needs another distraction. Plan B.

Sam ran to the second barn, crashing right through the old wooden door in a determined shoulder barge. He hastily pulled an old canvas cover from a shape in the corner. A car.

Bullitt.

Sam climbed in the driver's side and turned the key without hesitation. The old Mustang started up with a throaty roar. Sam gave the gas pedal a couple of little taps, selected *Drive* as he released the brake, and hit it.

Bullitt shot through the barn's old wooden doors like they were made of paper. Two Agents pursuing Tobias turned at the new sound.

Sam leaned on the horn. The Agents dived out of the way at the last moment as Sam roared past along the rough driveway, stirring up clouds of dust as he passed.

TINK!

The driver's side window cracked.

Stella. She stood in the middle of the paddock, her gun leveled at Sam.

TINK!

The windshield cracked. Sam slammed on the brakes and yanked the wheel hard to the right, almost doing a complete circle on the dusty path, throwing up billowing dust clouds. Facing Stella once more, now with two Agents by her side, coughing and squinting through the dust, but just as focused on Sam.

That's right, keep your eyes here.

TINK!

One of Stella's darts glanced off the cracked windshield.

Sam revved the engine. He looked past Stella to see Tobias climb the stairs to the aircraft, Duke slumped over his shoulder.

Gotta buy them just a little more time.

Sam slammed the accelerator to the floor. The back tires spun on the spot for a moment trying to get traction and creating another dust storm. Sam shot forward.

TINK! TINK! TINK!

Stella and her men held their ground and continued to fire at the approaching car.

The jet started up. The engines whining, burning hot.

Still Stella did not move, her eyes intent on Sam and the car speeding directly towards where she stood.

TINK! TINK!

The shattering windshield was a mass of cracks. Sam could barely see out as the darts flew thick and fast.

Sam kept his foot on the accelerator, building speed.

Almost there . . .

Stella and the Agents threw themselves out of the way as the Mustang raced past. Sam caught Stella's look of enraged frustration as she watched him go.

At the same moment, the jet rose vertically up into the sky, hovering above the ground and creating an immense dust storm over the farmhouse.

Plan B.

Tobias would keep the dust storm raging, obscuring the vision of Stella and her Agents while Sam got out to safety on the open road.

Sam was driving blind. But he knew that the way ahead was flat farmland and that it would be several minutes until he reached the gate down near the road, so he kept the steering wheel steady and drove in what he imagined was a straight line. He turned on his headlights to help him see, the light bouncing back at him from the dust in the air. The fuel gauge showed the tank was half full. Enough to get away.

Sam knew he wouldn't be stopping until he felt safe. Then he'd call the Academy and get help on the scene. Tobias' final words about Plan B rang in his ears.

Go down the driveway and don't look back. Follow the road out, get to the highway. Fast as you can. Remember to drive carefully through the tight corners—don't drift out on the gravel. I'll hold them off here, call for help and look after Duke.

You get yourself away, with the Gears, fast as you can—beat them to Cody and run, run, run.

The dust cleared and Sam finally pulled his foot back from the accelerator, just a fraction. He could see the fence up ahead. Not wanting to get out of the car, he nudged it closer to the old gate and slowed to a crawl. Instead of the chain snapping, the dry wooden posts on either side of the old metal gate pulled forward, coming out of the ground completely. Sam accelerated once more and drove over the wrecked gate, onto the gravel driveway, and then pulled out onto the road.

He took a glance back as he turned towards the highway. He could see the huge ball of dust, still glowing at its core from the house fire. By the swirling dust storm he could tell that the black jet still hovered up in the sky somewhere, but he could see no telltale signs of pursuing vehicles.

Not yet.

Sam squeezed his hands tighter on the steering wheel and steeled his nerves.

OK, no backpack means no phone and no money for more gas . . . but I have the Gears.

He took a final glance at the inferno in his rearview mirror before it disappeared from sight. Only a twist of dark-gray smoke curling into the afternoon sky over the horizon could be seen as Sam drove the Mustang east.

19

EVA

Lora was driving the Porsche Boxster like a race car driver.

"You really think the dealership believed you when you said you wanted to take this for a test drive?" Eva asked.

"Sure," Lora said. "They gave us the keys, didn't they?"

The highway ahead was nearly deserted and Lora let the sports car cruise at high speed.

"I'm sure they expected us to just go around the block a few times . . ." Eva said, shaking her head in disbelief. "I'll check in with Jedi for an update." Eva pulled out her phone.

The call was answered immediately back at the Academy. "Good timing," Jedi said over the speakerphone. "I've just tracked your location via your phone—whoa, you're really moving! Are you in an aircraft?"

"No, that's just Lora's driving," Eva said.

"Well, it's going to have to get pretty fancy," Jedi replied.

"Why's that?" Lora asked, wary.

"So," Jedi said, "you know how Mac's guys are on your tail?"

"Yeah, we know," Lora said, "though we haven't seen him and his gorillas for a while."

"Well," Jedi said, "you may be seeing them again soon. His gorillas are looking for you right now."

Eva looked at Lora as they both realized their suspicions about Mac were true. And if his men captured them again, they would be unlikely to get a second chance at freedom.

"How far out?" Lora asked, increasing the speed of the car even further along the empty highway. Eva held on tightly to her seat.

"Can't say exactly," Jedi replied. "Our Enterprise colleagues have also pointed out that Mac's got a lot of cool tech at play in his search for you."

"We'll outrun them," Lora replied, confident. "No one's going to get in our way and stop us from getting to Sam."

"Ah, yeah, you see that's going to be a problem," Jedi said. "On two fronts."

Jedi explained that he'd just heard from Tobias, and that he and Sam had had to split up in order to escape from Stella.

"Where is Sam now?" Eva asked.

"My satellite tracking has him headed across Texas towards the Arizona border. And Tobias is touching down the Enterprise aircraft in Houston. He is taking his uncle to the hospital and will then join up with a Guardian team to meet Sam."

"OK, we'll head there too," Lora said.

"And that other thing . . ." Jedi said, "the problem on the *other* front . . ."

"Yes?" Lora asked.

"It should be, ah, in your rearview mirror right about *now*."

Lora glanced in the mirror. Eva looked over her shoulder. A tiny glint was all that could be seen on the horizon.

"What *is* that?" Eva asked, straining to make it out.

Some kind of aircraft?

"I don't think we want to know!" Lora said.

There was very little fuel left in the Mustang's tank when Sam found a gas station. He pulled into a space near the pumps and turned off the engine, considering his options. It was late now, he didn't have any money to buy gas, and he was hungry and tired. He rummaged through the car and found a total of $2.85.

"Great," Sam said, looking at the change in his hand. "That'll get me two french fries and a couple of miles down the road."

He caught his reflection in the rearview mirror. He neatened up his hair and wiped some dirt from his cheek. Then, making sure that no one was looking, he changed the appearance of his Stealth Suit from the casual jeans and hoodie to a leather jacket, checked shirt and jeans.

I may be fifteen, but I can try my hardest not to look it.

He entered the diner next to the gas station and took a seat at the counter. With the money from the car, he bought a road map and a coffee, and waited for the pay phone to be free. The place was packed with truckers, and the smell of hamburgers and steaks sizzling made his stomach growl.

"More coffee, hon?" the waitress asked. She was a sweet-faced lady in her fifties, with ruddy cheeks and curly strawberry blond hair. Her name tag said "Flo."

"Yeah, thanks," Sam said. He added four sugars and a heap of milk to the steaming cup.

Looking at the map, Sam worked out that he was about fifty miles east of Albuquerque, roughly halfway between Amarillo and the Grand Canyon. If he somehow managed to fill Bullitt's tank, he could be there by daybreak.

Someone roared with laughter behind him and Sam nearly slipped off the chair in fright. His coffee spilled and he tried to mop it up with napkins, until Flo passed him a sponge. Sam turned to see a man laughing at a comic strip in the paper

It's just a guy, Sam. Relax, don't draw attention to yourself.

He looked around the diner, and out in the parking lot, for any suspicious faces. No one gave him a second glance as they ate their meals.

I need to call Lora, tell her everything, and see what she thinks I should do.

Sam absently looked out at the fuel pumps, then up at the underside of the roof covering the garage to see if there were any security cameras.

What are you thinking? No, don't steal gas.

Sam was lost in that thought for a moment, his mind trying to rationalize it out of desperation.

It'll only be about fifty bucks, and it is for the good of humanity.

"Headed to the Grand Canyon?" Flo asked, topping up his coffee again.

"Ah, yeah," Sam replied, stirred from his thoughts and looking down at the map where his finger rested on the dot that marked the tiny town of Forsyth. "Meeting a friend there."

"Hmm, nice time of year for it," Flo said. "Clear skies. Should see a lot."

"Yeah, I hope so," Sam said, sipping his coffee and looking again out to the car. The vintage Mustang was like a grandfather compared to the others out there, but it gleamed factory new.

How am I going to get money for gas . . ?

"That's your old '68?" Flo asked.

"It's—it's my uncle's," Sam said, figuring this wasn't such a lie since he looked at Tobias like an uncle, and it *was* Tobias' uncle's.

"She's a real beauty," Flo said. "1968 Mustang, made famous in the movie *Bullitt*, you know that, right? Will have to show my husband, he had one just like that when we met. Course, it wasn't a classic back then—practically brand new."

Sam nodded and smiled as she pointed out her husband through the kitchen window, a huge guy with a head like a smiling bulldog, expertly working the grill. The smell of the food made Sam's stomach groan again.

"Ah, I'll be back in a sec," Sam said, noting the pay phone

was now free. He picked up the receiver and called the Academy's emergency number.

"Academy," the voice said.

"This is Sam," he said quietly into the phone, not wanting to be overheard and looked at suspiciously by other diners. "Emergency field protocol Alpha."

The voice replied, "Copy that protocol Alpha, hold the line."

The sound changed to a different tone, and Sam could just imagine the call now being transferred from the London HQ to Lora's phone, via an array of satellites and microwave towers and through all sorts of security scramblers. It was a full minute before he heard the familiar voice say, "Sam?"

"Lora, I'm . . . I'm on the road," Sam said, wary, not wanting to give away too much detail over the phone. "I got separated from Tobias—he's running a diversion back at the farm in Amarillo."

"I heard, from Jedi," Lora replied. "He managed to get away with Duke. Are you OK?"

"I'm fine," Sam replied, recounting a short version of events that had led to him being here at the diner, halfway towards the next Dreamer, Cody.

"We'll head for you, and there is a team headed to Duke's farm to clean up the mess and make sure everything there is OK. Jedi is tracking you too, so a team of Guardians will be on your tail, ready if you need them."

"OK," Sam said, feeling a little better to hear his friend had survived Plan B and escaped all those armed thugs.

"Sam," Lora said, "how long do you think it will take you to get to Cody?"

"Well, that's just the thing . . . I left my wallet behind in my backpack, and I need to fill the car with gas."

There was silence on the other end of the phone, and then Lora said, "OK, let me talk to the owner. I'll pay over the phone with a credit card."

"Good idea, hang on," Sam said, then he went and got Flo, who spoke to Lora on the phone, then laughed heartily before passing the phone back to Sam.

"Wow, what'd you say?" Sam said to Lora.

"Just that I'm your big sister, and that you left your wallet at home, and that if your head wasn't screwed on you'd leave that behind too."

"That made her laugh like that?" Sam said.

"Well, I also added that last week you forgot to wear pants to school, and didn't realize the mistake until you were standing at your locker, wondering why there seemed to be such a breeze."

"Gee, thanks, way to embellish," Sam said, seeing now that Flo had told her husband and that he was looking at Sam and laughing too.

"OK, go fill the car and get to Cody," Lora said. "I'll split the Guardian team headed to Tobias and we'll come with the rest to get to you at the canyon. Stay safe."

"Thanks. And Lora?"

"Yeah?"

"Why do you sound like you're locked in some road race?"

"Don't ask," she replied. "Though it's nothing we can't handle."

"We?"

"Eva's here," Lora said.

"Hey, Sam—good luck!" Eva called out in the background.

"Thanks."

"Talk later," Lora said. "Got a little situation here."

"OK. Sounds like you guys need the good luck . . ." The phone call ended and Sam hung up the receiver, and sat back down to his map and coffee.

"This is on my husband," Flo said, putting a huge greasy hamburger down in front of Sam, along with a tall glass of soda. "Growing boy like you needs all the nourishment he can get."

It had taken Sam a lot longer than he'd hoped to get to Forsyth. He had been driving along the lonely highway, trying to keep his eyes open despite his fatigue. When he spotted a secluded area to the side of the road, he decided it was safer to pull over to sleep before continuing on.

When Sam exited the highway, a full twelve hours later than he had wanted, and drove towards Forsyth, the sun had almost completely disappeared. It was now just a red glow on the horizon. Bullitt's gas tank was nearly empty again. Sam pulled the Mustang over on the gravel shoulder of the road, came to a complete stop and turned off the engine, winding down his window. The sounds of crickets and critters called out in the coming nightfall. Sam breathed in clean, fresh air, and looked at the row of tired storefronts stretched out before him.

The first declared Forsyth's Souvenirs and Gift Shop "Closed," the second, Canyon View Motor and Tire Repairs, was the same. But it was the last that drew Sam's attention—CODY'S ADVENTURE TOURS.

All of it, exactly as his dream had shown.

With any luck, none of my dream was retrievable from Stella's broken dream machine.

Sam got out of the car and crunched his way across the pebbled driveway to the first store. The front door of Cody's tour company office was locked, so with hands cupped around his eyes, Sam peered through the glass. He couldn't see anyone inside the dark room.

Maybe I'm too late . . . it's much later than my dream, maybe Cody's gone home for the day.

Sam headed around the back of the building, trying to be quiet on the gravel, stopping to listen at the next corner. His eyes had adjusted to the dim light, and he could make out a figure moving around in front of a well-lit storage garage.

It was a tall man, strapping kayaks onto a trailer. As Sam neared, he could make out more details.

Cody.

Sam walked towards him.

"Hey," Cody said, turning at the noise and seeing Sam. "How's it going?"

"Hi," Sam said. He joined him at the garage. "Good. You?"

"You know, just packing up, getting ready for tomorrow." Cody leaned back on tie-down straps to tighten them. He looked about eighteen or so, but was much bigger than Sam—at least six foot four, muscular, with blond hair sticking out from under a trucker's cap. He had bright-blue eyes and gleaming white teeth that flashed against his well-tanned skin.

"Yeah, so I see . . ."

Cody smiled. "I head out early mornings, and tomorrow's booked out, if you're looking for a tour."

"That's cool," Sam said. "Besides, I'm not much of a fan of early mornings."

A cool breeze against the back of his neck gave him a chill and he looked around, startled.

"You lost or something?" Cody asked, looking at Sam.

"Nope."

"Well, if you're looking for a tour, you'll need to call in the morning and arrange another time."

"Yeah . . ." Sam said distractedly.

"*Are* you looking for a tour?" Cody asked, wiping his dusty hands on his jeans.

"Well, of sorts," Sam replied.

Cody frowned, shrugged, then finished loading the final kayak. He stopped and looked at Sam closely.

"I'm Sam," Sam introduced himself, hand outstretched.

"Cody."

"Yeah. So, busy day tomorrow then."

"Yep. Good weather forecast, plenty of folk around this time of year."

"Don't suppose you can cancel, for a private tour?"

Cody looked at Sam, his head tilted slightly sideways and a grin forming. "That'd cost you. Have to get another hand at short notice to cover my shift."

"I have plenty of money," Sam said, thinking he could

place another call to Lora for payment if it came to it, or, better yet, he could convince Cody in the meantime that he was one of the last 13, holding the fate of the whole world in his subconscious . . .

Surely he wouldn't charge me then.

"What kind of tour do you have in mind?" Cody asked.

"A flyover of the canyon."

Cody shook his head. "Sorry, I don't do flights. You gotta go another ten miles up the highway for that. Got helicopter and aircraft tours up there." He could see that Sam was disappointed.

"You don't take flights?" Sam said. "You see, time is kind of, ah, of the essence."

Cody shook his head again, emphatic this time.

"Not even in ultralights?" Sam asked. "Or powered gliders?"

"Nope. Nothing powered. We do trekking by foot, rock-climbing, kayaks, riverboarding and spelunking only."

"Riverboarding?"

"White-water rafting—without the raft. Just a life jacket, padding, a helmet and one of these little boards."

"Right," Sam said, his voice trailing off on seeing the tiny bodyboard-type raft.

This is the guy—trust the dream. We'll kayak there, like we did in the dream . . . I guess no changing things this time.

"You OK?" Cody asked.

"Yeah, totally." Sam smiled.

"Good for you. Catch you tomorrow, maybe," Cody said, and walked across the driveway into the back of his office.

"Cody, can we talk for a sec?" Sam said, catching up with him. "I really need to talk to you about something."

"We open at 6 a.m. tomorrow—"

"That's fine. We can head out then. I want to go to a place where there's a fork in the canyon."

"Oh right, well, that narrows it down." Cody gave a loud laugh.

"And there's a hidden secret there. With a drawing, a very particular drawing. Thirteen figures?"

Cody stopped and spun around to look at him cautiously. "Where'd you hear about such a place?"

"The Internet."

Cody scoffed. "It's not on the Internet."

"But there is such a place?"

Cody remained silent, looking like he'd realized he had said too much already. Then he said, "That site's secret. Nobody other than the local custodians know of it."

"Perhaps I didn't introduce myself properly before," Sam said. "But just get me to the canyon tomorrow morning and I will explain everything."

Cody looked at Sam, weighing up what he'd said. "So if I take you there, you'll tell me how you heard about it?"

"Yeah."

"Getting there in a kayak ain't no picnic."

"I know." Sam swallowed hard as he thought back to

the smashed kayak of his dream.

Cody looked at him with a little grin forming at the corners of his mouth. "You done white water before?"

"Nope."

"You staying up the road, in town?" Cody asked.

"No. Nothing planned yet," Sam replied.

"We got a couple of rooms, nothing fancy but our workers stay there, you're welcome to them."

"Thanks, that would be great."

"Follow me."

Sam followed him up the hill to a little house looking down at the road and parking lot next to the garage. They went around the back, to where a clutch of little bungalows ringed a wide lawn with a swimming pool in the center.

"I wouldn't recommend taking a swim in the dark. You can't check for snakes," Cody said. He opened the door to the first bungalow. The room inside was decked floor to ceiling with Native American art and artifacts. He opened a small bar fridge in the far corner and poured a couple of cold drinks.

"So tell me, how'd you know about the building, the temple, and that drawing?" Cody asked. He looked around, as though there was some great conspiracy afoot.

"You *showed* me," Sam said, smiling.

"What are you talking about? I've *shown* no one! I've not even told anyone."

Sam smiled. "Not even in a dream?"

22

EVA

"**W**e have to get off the road!" Eva said, doing her best to locate their pursuer through the open side window.

"Can you see it?"

"No," Eva said. "Wait—yes! It's up there, following every move we make."

High above them was an aircraft, following every evasive maneuver that Lora tried. Nothing seemed to work. The small plane looped around and through the sky after them.

"I'm doing my best!" Lora said, navigating through the smaller roads off the highway.

"What is it?" Eva had never seen anything like it.

"An Unmanned Aerial Vehicle—a UAV," Lora explained. "A drone aircraft, remote controlled."

"Well, it's not going anywhere," Eva said, watching it above them. "If we don't lose it, it'll track us all the way to Sam. How long can it stay up there?"

"If it's high-tech? Hours," Lora said. "And it's able to travel way faster than any car."

"Great. Is it armed?"

"Doubt it—too small. Observation only," Lora said. "They want to know where we're going."

"Stella, Hans or Mac?"

I can't believe I'm reeling off a list of enemies now!

"No way of knowing. But we can't lead it to Sam."

"Then what do we do?"

"Outsmart it," Lora said with a grim smile.

"Do you think this UAV thing can follow us in the dark?" Eva said. She'd not seen it for hours, even when they'd stopped to refuel the car and get food.

"Yep, easily," Lora said, driving the Porsche at a steady speed among the highway traffic. "It will be equipped with infrared, so it's locked on to this car. Might even have a way of tracing us through the Academy's mobile phones."

Eva looked at the phone on her lap that she'd used several times to contact Jedi. They'd driven from Washington State, down through Oregon and California, through to Death Valley. Now they were approaching a big glow on the horizon.

"We're going to ditch everything up here," Lora said.

"What's up here?" Eva looked around. They were in desert country. There was not much of anything around, but plenty of cars traveling on the highway.

"Big hotels," Lora said. "And even bigger crowds. Big, bright and so busy that we might be able to ditch this aircraft too."

Eva nodded, though she felt tired and apprehensive. She stared at a garish road sign up ahead, welcoming them to "fabulous" Las Vegas.

SAM

"**M**aybe I kind of always knew," Cody said, heating up a huge pot of chili with beef and beans over a fire pit in a rocky campsite behind the bungalows. "All of my life, I've dreamed big. And the last few months, my dreams have become more and more vivid . . ."

"Well, I'm here to tell you that you're not alone," Sam said. "There's many of us, always have been."

"Dreamers?"

"Yep, that's what they call us. And you and I, we're part of a particular group—perhaps even more gifted than the others—who need to come together in order to retrieve something very important. There are 13 of us, and we are the best shot at winning this race for good."

"Gifted?" Cody asked. "Compared to who? And what, will I become, like, stronger and faster? Like a superhero?"

Sam shook his head and laughed.

"Afraid not, least not in the real, waking world," Sam said. He was leaning back on a camp chair, far from the small crackling fire. "But we have the ability to control our dreams—and our dreams are true dreams. They offer glimpses into the future."

"Right," Cody said, nodding as Sam spoke. "That's how I found the temple in the first place. I'd dreamed about gliding down a gorge, and then kayaking until I found it. And the next day, I did it."

"When was that?" Sam asked, trying to conceal his nervousness.

How long a jump might we have on everyone else coming after us?

"Three days ago. At first I thought it just a dream. Then, the next night, bam! Another dream—same place, but more detail. Then it felt like I had to go. I thought it was crazy, but I just couldn't not. Does that make sense?"

Sam nodded. "And so then you went there . . ." he prompted.

"Yep. And it was exactly as I'd dreamed. Well, that and more. It's phenomenal."

"And what did you find?"

Cody's eyes lit up. He went into his bungalow and came back with a small box, which he opened next to Sam. Cody carefully unwrapped the linen cloths inside to reveal two small animal statues made from clay.

"They're old, really old," Cody said. "The temple looks like it was made by ancient Puebloan people, hundreds of years ago, if not more."

"Nothing else?" Sam asked, almost apologetically.

Cody shook his head. "But, there's plenty of these there," he said. "I photographed the area where I found the statues. There's a huge collection of them near the entrance. Like I said, I only went to the site two days ago—that's why I was so shocked when you mentioned it. I can't believe you've seen it in your dream too. That's wild!"

"You said it," Sam said. "Hey, can I use your phone?"

"Sure," Cody said, pointing towards the open back door of the bungalow. "It's on the counter."

Sam went inside and phoned Lora. He called Cody in, then put the phone on speaker and made the introductions.

"The Guardians are about three hours away from Tobias," Lora said. "They've had to shake a tail."

"Guardians protect Dreamers," Sam said to Cody by way of explanation. Then he said to Lora, "Was it Hans following them?"

"We don't know."

"Who's Hans?" Cody asked.

"Billionaire treasure hunter, and he's got the German Guardians backing him," Sam replied. "He wants what we know and have."

"To get the Gears and build da Vinci's Bakhu machine."

"Yep."

"Which is really a mechanical map," Cody said, "that will reveal the location of the Dream Gate."

"Wow, you're a quick learner, Cody," Lora said over the

speakerphone. "Took Sam ages to get his head around all that."

Sam could hear the humor in her voice. "Yeah, yeah," he said.

"It all makes sense . . ." Cody said, leaning on the counter towards the phone. "It feels like I've been expecting this. Thirteen of us . . ."

"Tobias and the Guardians will be at your location by sunrise," Lora said.

"We'll be waiting," Sam replied.

"Meanwhile," she added, "if you're OK, we'll change our plans and go see about a site that Mac may be using as a base. See if we can't put him out of business."

"Good luck with that," Sam replied.

"What kind of security is there?" Lora asked.

"We're safe," Cody replied. "We're at my house, about fifteen minutes from the canyon entrance that I always use."

"Which is what I saw in my dream," Sam added. "My worry is that with Stella on our tail, she might also be headed there. I mean, I wrecked her dream recorder, but I can't help feeling that she'll find out where we're going . . ." He trailed off.

"Sam?" Lora said.

"It's nothing. Just memories from my dream. We'll hunker down here until sunrise. Hopefully Tobias will be here by then."

"Hang on," Lora said. "Cody, do you live alone?"

"No," Cody replied. "This is my parents' place."

Lora was silent for a moment and Sam knew what was coming. He had yet to tell Cody that there was the possibility his parents may not be who they seemed. He looked up from the kitchen counter and scanned the room, as though there may be eavesdroppers.

"Where are your parents now?" Sam asked.

"They left a couple of days ago," Cody said. "They went to the university in Tucson for work. They won't be back until the middle of next week."

"OK, well that's one less complication to worry about. You should be safe there," Lora said. "But, Sam, maybe don't stay at the house tonight, just in case Stella knows more than we'd like."

"Complication? Stella?" Cody asked. "What's going on?"

"I'll explain later," Sam said, peering through the blinds to the empty road and parking lot at the back of the stores down below. "But we should probably camp somewhere."

Sam and Cody sat around the new campfire. Cody had been silent since Sam had told him about the possibility that his parents were Agents for the Enterprise. And of the possibility that some surrogate parents may also have defected to Stella's side. Sam understood—it was a shock to think that everything in life was not as it had always appeared to be.

Sam looked up at the sky. It was a clear night and the air was cool. The campfire was just low embers now, which glowed dimly with intense heat. They were over a gully and up the hill from Cody's house. If they walked for a minute to the ridge, they could see the bungalows and the road that branched off the main street and led to the tour office.

"I just can't believe it," Cody said, absently stirring the pot of chili they'd hauled up with them. "I really can't."

"Look, try not to think about it—they may not even be Agents. I know it's hard to take in, but if they have been away for the last few days and don't know about the dreams you've had, then we have no need to worry. We can sort it all out later."

"Why can't I just contact them—ask them directly myself?" Cody asked, holding up his phone.

"Ah, that's not a great idea just now," Sam said. "We need to make sure we get to the Gear first. Agents or not, if Stella has a way of tracing their phone calls, she might track them down too. We don't want to put them in danger unnecessarily."

Cody didn't say anything but he served up two bowls of the steaming chili and they sat and ate in silence.

"Holy smoke!" Sam said, fanning his mouth. "This is hot as!" His eyes started watering and he ate a chunk of cornbread and washed it down with a swift gulp of milk.

"OK, a little hot, but totally awesome," he said, eating more.

Cody didn't seem fazed by the spicy food. He looked as though a thought was just dawning on him.

"What is it?" Sam asked.

"In this place, hidden in the canyons," Cody said, "there's that carving showing thirteen figures together. Do you think that could be a depiction of opening the Dream Gate?"

Sam nodded thoughtfully.

"And you know what else?" Cody said.

Sam waited as Cody had a drink of milk—maybe the chili was finally getting to him, too.

"I found some skeletons. Three of them," Cody said. "Spanish, I think, by their clothing and gear. Sixteenth century, some of the first European explorers through this area. I didn't touch any of the artifacts—I just saw them and raced back. But they'd not been disturbed, I know, because one of them had some gold coins spilled on the ground from a little pouch—I mean, if anyone else had found it, they'd have taken them, right?"

"And you haven't been back there since?" Sam asked.

"After finding those Spanish skeletons, I was kinda spooked," Cody said, finishing off his bowl of chili and serving up seconds.

"Well," Sam said, looking at their sleeping bags rolled out under the sky of brilliant stars above, "tomorrow's the day. You and I will find it again and get some real answers."

ALEX

Alex walked briskly in the cold night, Phoebe in step beside him. Their Stealth Suits had changed to appear as the uniforms of the Washington, DC, Police Department.

"Do I look too young to be a cop?" Alex asked.

"I hope you'll always look too young to be a cop," his mother replied, pinching his cheek.

"Ah, Mom!" he said, rubbing where she'd squeezed and looking around to make sure no one had noticed.

"Come on, let's check the Metro station," Phoebe said, stepping up the pace so that Alex had to jog to catch up with her.

"But there's a team of Agents staking that out!" Alex said, protesting. "Can't we have a break to grab a bite to eat? I'm starving!"

"Sure," Phoebe said, not breaking her stride. "Who really wants to save the world anyway?"

"Argh, I knew being keen to get involved would come back to bite me," Alex said, kicking at the ground. "Fine, we'll go to the Metro. There'll at least be a vending machine down there."

"You don't need anything that'll rot your teeth," Phoebe said.

"Yeah, Mom, I know . . ." They strode across the National Mall, and he stopped to look up at the towering obelisk of the Washington Monument.

"Beautiful, isn't it?" Phoebe said.

"Yeah, I guess," Alex said. "But, like almost everything I've seen so far, it's hiding its true purpose."

Alex yawned. They'd been up all night without so much as a jaywalker in sight. Aside from them, there were twelve of the best Enterprise Agents in the area, in the two-person patrols disguised as police, scouring for any sight of Mac or Stella.

So far, nothing.

"Well, that was boring," Alex said, yawning again.

"What, hanging out with your mother all night on a mission to save the world?"

"Ah, I'm too tired to argue, Mom, so I'll take it back. It's been a blast walking around the National Mall with you in the middle of the night."

"Better." Phoebe smiled.

Alex looked around. "When's this changeover shift coming?"

"They're late," Phoebe said. "They were meant to meet up with us half an hour ago."

"Why didn't you tell me?"

"I didn't want to worry you," she said. "Let me call them again." She was about to make a call on her radio when she saw a little coffee van serving cab drivers at a street corner a couple of blocks down. "Hey, would you please get me a coffee? I'll wait here in case they turn up."

"Sure, be right back," Alex said, and he jogged across the Mall and ordered a couple of double-shot espressos and some food. He paid the guy and walked back to where his mother had been standing—but she was gone. He spun around, immediately anxious.

Nothing. Plenty of people, but no Phoebe—no cops at

all. He called into his radio, a closed circuit used only by them and the Agents, but got no reply.

Nothing at all.

"Mom!" he called out loud. "Phoebe!"

His shouts startled a flock of pigeons and some Japanese tourists walking past him. One of them handed him a DC police badge, pointed up the Mall a few yards, towards the Washington Monument, miming that they'd found it on the ground. He thanked them, and saw on the inscription that it was his mother's—like the utility belt that they wore, loaded with handcuffs, flashlight, and pistol, the badge was authentic enough so that they passed as regular DC cops, but not quite right on closer inspection. He dropped the food and drinks and ran towards the towering obelisk.

SAM

"No! No!"

Sam woke. By the light of the night sky and the still glowing coals of the campfire he could see Cody murmuring and twitching in his sleep.

Strange. I can't even remember if I just dreamed or not.

Sam thought about waking him, and then decided not to. Better to let him sleep, finish the dream he was obviously having.

Wait until he wakes and see what he's dreamed—with any luck, it'll show us exactly where we have to go.

Sam yawned and rolled back over in his sleeping bag.

CODY'S NIGHTMARE

I look up, following the noise. It's a huge A380 coming in for landing. My eyes are distracted by–*a horse?*

It's a great big stallion, rearing up on its hind legs, its veins snaking around its body, its eyes shining red, terrifying.

It doesn't move.

I come nearer.

A statue. It's just a statue . . .

"Cody!"

I turn at the sound of my name.

Sam.

"Come on!" Sam calls, and I run after him through the main terminal of the large airport. We stop at a door marked, SECURITY PERSONNEL ONLY.

Sam enters a code into the keypad—130107.

The light on the lock bleeps green and the door clicks open. A long corridor lights up before us as we run through it.

"What's the rush?" I ask, but then the answer comes—

"Hey, you!" A security guard appears from a side hall.

Sam doesn't hesitate or skip a beat—he's on the guy, flipping him onto his back and knocking him out with one swift movement.

"We don't have much time," Sam says. "Let's go."

"Where?"

Sam stops. "This is your show," he says to me.

We both stop. There, in front of me, is the black horse again. It towers over us, its eyes glowing bright red. I can make out a low growling sound, and turn my head trying to pinpoint where the noise is coming from. Suddenly the imposing black horse breathes fire at us.

"Down!" Sam pulls me to the floor and we crawl to the other side of the hall. "That's him!"

"Who?"

"Solaris," Sam yells out.

"The horse?"

"What horse?" he says.

"You didn't see the horse?" I don't understand.

Sam shakes his head. We hear footsteps approaching, they're loud echoes on the polished concrete floor. A tall figure, dark and shadowy, makes his way towards us. His movement looks unnatural.

"Leave us alone!" Sam yells at the guy, getting to his feet and looking defiant.

The figure shoots flames towards Sam. I can see Sam freeze, before recoiling back. The metallic voice behind the mask cackles, satisfied.

"Sam . . ." Solaris says with a voice distorted and amplified. I cover my ears. "Who's your friend?"

"Go away!" Sam says to him, standing between me and this terrifying apparition. I want to help, I think of crash-tackling him, but my feet feel locked to the floor. His shimmering mass looks as if it could shift at the slightest movement.

"You know I will follow you anywhere you try to hide," Solaris says. "When you dream, any of you, you're in my world."

Sam is silent.

"What do you want with us?" I ask.

I feel Solaris move his gaze to look at me with his black eyes.

"The Gear," Solaris says, and then in a blur of motion he has Sam in a choke hold. He picks him up by his neck and turns him around, so that Sam, feet off the floor, is now facing me. His hands fight uselessly against Solaris' grip.

"The Gear," Solaris says again. "It's here. Give it to me."

"Don't do it!" Sam manages to blurt out.

"Sam . . . always the hero . . ." Solaris brings his other arm up, his wrist towards Sam's face, and makes the tiny flame larger, burning like a blowtorch in front of Sam's eyes.

Sam looks terrified. He closes his eyes tight and everything turns to white in one blinding flash.

SAM

"**A**nd that was it?" Sam asked, his teeth chattering against the morning chill in the air, the sun yet to appear over the horizon. Cody was checking over their kayaks and equipment. "That was the extent of your dream?"

"Yep. Thanks again for waking me," Cody said. "I think we're good to go."

"So, an airport . . . I wonder why we were there?" Sam said. Cody explained that the beginning of the dream had been the same as before—the canyon and the rock carvings and the hidden temple. But then it had abruptly changed setting.

"Beats me," Cody said. "It was a big airport, and one I'd never seen. And that massive black horse with crazy eyes . . . it was a weird dream."

"Yeah," Sam said. "They sometimes are."

"The same thing happens to you?"

"I . . . I keep having these dreams of a desert—not at all like this one here, just endless sand dunes, and I'm with a friend, Alex. But the dream just shows me little snippets.

It's all broken up, a glimpse here and there. None of it makes sense, but none of it is good for me or Alex either."

"Is Alex another Dreamer?"

"Yeah."

"What do you think it means?"

"I don't know . . . OK, so how do we get down *there?*" Sam asked, suddenly eager to change the topic. He pointed to a brilliant blue-green stream a couple of hundred yards below the parking lot. The water seemed to originate at the base of a cliff, where an underground aquifer roared out into the open and foamed like a shaken can of soda.

A million cans of soda more like.

"We BASE jump," Cody said, matter-of-fact.

"That's . . . interesting," Sam said, his voice edgy. "But how do the kayaks get down there?"

"We sit in them."

"I don't follow," Sam said.

"We strap in," Cody explained, "and then we push off."

Sam looked over the edge of the sheer cliff. "And *land* in the water in our kayaks?"

"That's it," Cody said. "So technically we don't jump, we just kind of line ourselves up near the edge and then— whoosh, off we go. Cool, huh?"

Sam swallowed hard and strapped on the parachute Cody handed to him. Cody checked the straps, then Sam reciprocated with a cross-check, before checking his own again nervously.

"You ever skydived or BASE jumped?" Cody asked.

"Yeah, once or twice," Sam said, thinking back to how he'd turned his Stealth Suit into an improvised glider to escape from Solaris at the top of the Eiffel Tower, and again with Rapha in the jungle. "It's not an activity I'm in a hurry to repeat . . ."

"You're gonna love this, Sammy!" Cody was all smiles. "It's a blast!"

"Yeah . . ." Sam nodded. "Let's, ah, let's do this!"

Cody slapped him on the shoulder and then helped him into the kayak.

"Me first," Cody said, getting into his own craft. "Count to three, then follow my lead. When we land on the river, keep the canopy up until we reach the first junction—it'll work like a power sail as the wind's ripping through the canyon behind us. Then ditch it and switch to the paddle to get to shore."

"Where's that exactly?" Sam asked, squinting his eyes to see down to the tiny little river far below.

"Can't see it from here, but just follow me, OK?"

Sam nodded, tightened his helmet strap and made sure the paddle was clipped securely to the kayak's side.

"Hang on, why the first junction?" Sam asked.

"It's too turbulent from that point on, so we have to paddle."

"How far?"

Cody smiled. "Not that far. You ready?"

"As I'll ever be."

Cody wriggled back and forth and his kayak started sliding along the loose dusty ground and down the steep slope until—

He disappeared.

"Hee-yaaaaa!" Sam could hear Cody call over the microphone headset he was wearing, although Cody was so loud he would have heard him clearly without it.

"OK, ancient prophecy," Sam said aloud. "I'm trusting that this is what I'm meant to be doing, so I really hope this works."

He rocked back and forth quickly, just as Cody had done, and in seconds he'd slid away from the sloped ground and out over the edge of the cliff—

"Arghhhhh!"

"Sam? Sam!"

Sam sat up, coughing and spluttering water.

"Are you OK?" Cody asked.

Sam nodded and wiped the water from his face. The two of them were on the sandy riverbank. Only Cody's kayak was visible.

"You . . . did you just give me mouth-to-mouth?" Sam asked, struggling to focus against the bright light of the morning.

"No," Cody laughed. "I just cleared out your airway and you started heaving out water."

"Thanks," Sam said. "How'd I get out of the river?"

"That outfit you're wearing," Cody said, pointing to Sam's Stealth Suit. "After you caught an updraft and crashed into the canyon wall and into the water, I thought you were a goner. But then you bobbed up, floating like a cork—wearing the biggest full-body life vest I've ever seen."

Sam looked down and saw that the suit had morphed into an inflated coverall.

Latest gen Stealth Suit . . . thanks, Jedi.

"I glided to the river about five hundred yards downstream from where you were, and waited for you to float down," Cody said. "You came past and I pulled you ashore."

"Thanks," Sam replied, then stood on wobbly legs and changed his Stealth Suit back to the survival-type gear he'd started out the day with.

"Whoa! That's pretty cool."

"Yeah, they'll give you one of these suits when you go to the Academy," Sam said. He looked back at the river. "My kayak?"

Cody pointed a thumb downstream. "Floated away, I'm afraid. I'll be billing you for that later," he laughed coarsely.

Sam looked at Cody's kayak. There was no way that the two of them could ride in it and keep it afloat. "So what now?" he said.

"We hoof it," Cody said. "I'll leave my kayak here. The

temple is still a couple of clicks downriver. We should be able to follow the river's edge, but we'll probably have to do some serious rock climbing over these boulders."

"OK, let's do it."

Sam followed Cody and the first few hundred yards were easy going, until they came to a sheer cliff face at which point they had no choice but to jump into the river. They floated along, and then Cody was first to shore about a hundred yards down, pulling Sam up onto a rocky ledge.

"Argh!" Sam jumped up from where he'd been seated, catching his breath.

"What?"

"*That!*" Sam pointed to a large scorpion close to his shoe. It was almost the same size, light-yellow in color and with huge, lobster-like pincers.

"He's fine. Stomp near him and he'll run away."

"Poisonous?"

"A little, wouldn't hurt much more than a bee sting, though."

"Yeah, well I think I'm more worried about him carrying me off limb by limb." Sam stamped his boot and the creature scuttled into a gap between the rocks.

Cody laughed.

"Gee, he's got like his own lair down there." Sam shuddered as he peered into the crevasse. "Anything else out here gonna eat me?"

"Not much will want to eat you out here—least, not while you're alive," Cody said, pressing on.

"Huh?"

"I mean nothing will attack you. But if you were a rotting corpse, that'd be a different story. Then all kinds of animals would come for a feed. Eagles, condors, mountain lions . . ."

"Sounds great," Sam mumbled. "Must remember not to become a rotting corpse down here."

ALEX

Alex stood inside the maintenance area of the Washington Monument. A sign said it was closed to the public pending an engineer's safety inspection due to renovations and maintenance. There was a site room with a few empty desks, and with no one in sight, Alex called the Enterprise's emergency number and asked for the director.

"He's unavailable," the operator replied.

"Shiva," Alex said. "Put me through to Shiva."

"Please hold."

Alex used the time to catch his breath.

"Yo, this is Shiva," the familiar voice said.

"Shiva, it's Alex—"

"Hey, man, how goes it?"

"I've got an emergency here," Alex said, explaining the mysterious disappearance of his mother and the other Agents.

"You've had no contact with any of them for how long?"

"A while," Alex hedged. "But I've looked everywhere."

"Why didn't you call in sooner?"

"I wanted to see if I could figure out what was going

on," Alex said, feeling a bit dumb about it now. "I thought I could fix this—whatever *this* is."

"OK. You're at the Washington Monument now?"

"Yep."

"All right, look," Shiva said, "leave Phoebe and the others to me. I'll direct whatever resources we've got in the area to you so we can find them."

"OK, thanks."

"Meantime, this changes everything—your mission there is now no longer one of waiting and watching to see if anyone turns up."

"What is it now?" Alex asked.

"You're going to have to make sure that the Washington Monument is shut down."

"Shut down? What do you mean?"

"I mean take it out of operation so that Mac or Stella or whoever can't get it operational."

"And how exactly do I do that?"

"I'm working on it," Shiva said. "OK, here, I've got the schematics in front of me. You need to get to the top and disconnect the transceiver."

"And where's that?"

"It'll be in the pyramidion—the point at the top of the Monument. There's an access hatch near to it. Go through that and then you'll see an aluminum apex that forms the capstone. Pry it open and disconnect all the wiring."

"Like, just unplug it?"

"Well, it'd be a lot better if you could take it out of action more, shall we say, *permanently.*"

"I'm not going to *destroy* the Washington Monument!" Alex exclaimed.

"No, geez, I mean just cut any wires you find. Rip it all apart, rather than just switch it off," Shiva said. "That'll buy us time until we get a tech out there to disable it for good."

"So you want me to get to the top of the world's tallest obelisk and wreak whatever havoc I can on whatever tech I find under the capstone, all the while avoiding capture."

"Sounds about right. Oh, and I'd be wary of the winds up there—wouldn't want to get blown off from 500 feet. We'd have to send cleaners to scrape your remains off the Mall."

"Gee, thanks, you're a pal," Alex said.

"Hey, *you* wanted to be part of this race. Now's your chance."

"Yeah, yeah, well you just find my mother and the others. Talk to you on the flip side."

Alex ended the call and headed into the subbasement and pressed the elevator call button. *Least there's an elevator . . .*

Then he noticed the sign:

ELEVATOR OUT OF ORDER—

TAKE THE STAIRS, ALL 897 OF THEM!

"Ha, big joke . . ." Alex said, putting his foot on the first step.

EVA

"**N**O!" Eva said, sitting up, startled, looking at Lora who'd shaken her awake.

"You were asleep," Lora said. "Talking in your sleep."

Eva nodded. "Where are we?"

"Las Vegas, in our hotel. We walked here after ditching the car and our phones in that underground parking garage on the other side of town, remember?"

Eva sat motionless and unresponsive on the bed, looking out at the view.

"Eva? What's the matter?" Lora asked, concerned about the expression on Eva's frozen face.

"I was having a nightmare . . . about Sam. He's in trouble!"

"What kind of trouble?"

"He's . . ." Eva breathed deeply. "He and Cody. They're walking into a trap!"

"Are you sure? We've got no way of contacting them. Sam doesn't have his phone, and they'll already be headed to the Gear location."

"Cody has a phone," Eva countered.

"You're sure?" Lora asked again.

"He did in my dream."

"That's good enough for me. Get dressed, and we'll find a pay phone and place a call."

"Pay phone?" Eva asked, slipping into her Stealth Suit which then changed into a black-and-white dress.

"We may have given that drone the slip when we ditched the car," Lora said, hurriedly packing up their small collection of things. "But as soon as we place a call to Cody or the Academy, I'm sure they'll track our location. Let's be on our way out in case they have people move in."

"OK," Eva said, still shaken. They headed out the door.

In the lobby of the hotel they found a row of pay phones to the side of the reception area.

"Eva, you keep a lookout," Lora said, then punched in Jedi's number. Lora sounded serious as she spoke to him, her words tumbling out quickly one after the other. In under two minutes the conversation was over and they were walking out of the lobby doors. "Jedi is trying to get through to Sam to warn him."

Lora flagged a taxi and held the back door open for Eva.

"Meanwhile, we'll either charter a helicopter to get to Sam or . . ." Lora's voice trailed off as Eva climbed into the backseat of the cab.

Two black cars roared to an abrupt stop at one end of the hotel's circular driveway, about six taxis behind them. Several big guys, all wearing suits, scrambled out.

Lora jumped into the front passenger seat of the taxi.

"Drive!" she yelled at the driver, who looked from the two of them to the group of guys headed their way.

"Sorry, lady, I don't want any trouble with the law," the driver replied. Then he switched off the engine, opened his door and climbed out, waiting for Lora and Eva to do the same.

"Do they look like the law to you?" Lora yelled, not moving from her seat.

Eva dived into the driver's seat, started up the taxi and took off in a cloud of tire smoke. "Hang on!" she yelled as she did a sudden U-turn across six lanes of traffic. The rear of the cab clipped two others waiting in a rank, before continuing down the busy road. Once she had steadied the taxi, Eva pressed down harder on the gas. "Where should I go?"

"Another hotel!" Lora said, then pointed. "Take that right, pull into the biggest casino complex you can see, and we'll lose them inside."

"Got it!" Eva kept her foot to the floor, seeing the two black cars in pursuit just as she rounded the corner.

"That one!" Lora said, pointing to a huge glittering glass hotel and casino across the road.

Eva pulled into the driveway and parked the car behind

the other taxis dropping off and picking up patrons and guests. They jumped out of their taxi, not stopping to even close the doors behind them and ran inside the casino. As they entered the lobby, they changed their Stealth Suits to resemble the uniforms of the staff members they saw walking by.

"Rear exit," Lora said. "Head for the restaurants and we'll go through the kitchens and out the back."

"Follow me," Eva said, spying a sign for the dining room.

They could hear the sound of a commotion breaking out behind them. Eva turned quickly to see six suited men arguing with the casino's security. The security guards refused them entry.

Lora smiled at Eva as they walked quickly side by side.

"That was some nice work," she said. "At this rate, you're going to have me out of a job."

29

SAM

An hour later, after much walking and scrambling over jagged rocks, they arrived at the fork in the river. Sam immediately felt as if he were reliving his dream.

"Impressive, huh?" Cody said.

A wedge-shaped canyon wall towered above them. Set within it, hidden except from this specific angle, there stood the entrance to a temple, carved into the rock. They waded across the river, grasping at overhanging branches for support, paddling across the current. At the far shore, they walked up to the entrance, Sam wide-eyed in wonder.

"Why would someone have built this here?" Sam asked, touching a stone pillar that had the faded tracings of snakes wrapped around it.

"I don't know," Cody said, drinking from a water bottle. "I know the whole region has artifacts dating to the Iron Age, some up to 4000 years old. The Puebloans built heaps of stone and mud structures, especially into cliffs and caves like this, though I've never seen anything this detailed."

They began to make their way up the slope of centuries' worth of rubble that had eroded from the canyon wall. It was like walking up a small sand dune.

"Well, this Gear that we are after?" Sam said. "Most of the Gears we have found so far seem to date from the early 1500s onward."

"Sounds like about the right period for those Spanish skeletons."

"Exactly. It'll probably be near them," Sam said, thinking back to his time with Rapha in the hidden city of the Cloud People. Then he frowned. "It's weird, though . . ."

"What is?" Cody said stopping suddenly.

"That you haven't seen the Gear in your dream," Sam said. "I've only just really realized. It all felt right, and it matched *my* dream exactly, so I just assumed that you had."

"That's what usually happens?"

"Yep. Up till now it's always been the same—I dream of the Dreamer, the Dreamer dreams of the Gear."

"Maybe it's changed somehow," Cody said. "I mean,

as I was dreaming, maybe it's been moved."

"Moved? Maybe, I guess."

We'll find out soon enough . . .

Sam paused at the tunnel entrance, feeling a wave of anxiety stirring within him. Debris blocked most of the way in, leaving no more than a tight crawl space to enter the temple beyond.

He shrugged. "We're here now. Let's do this."

"Lights on," Cody said, switching on the bright LED flashlight on his helmet. "Watch out for the drop at the end."

"Huh?" Before Sam could make sense of the warning, Cody had slid down the other side. Thankfully, seeing him down there and watching the path of his light down the steep drop, Sam knew what was ahead. He switched on his own light and then slid down.

"Oww!" Sam hit hard, then looked up and got a fright.

Saber-toothed tigers carved from the stone stood menacingly outside the door.

"Reckon they were based on real creatures?" Sam asked.

"What, like around when this place was built?" Cody said.

Sam nodded.

"Doubt it. Saber-tooths come from a real long time ago—certainly not a time you'd associate with such fancy building work. Could be that different parts have been added on over time."

"Well, we should watch where we step," Sam cautioned.

"What are you saying?" Cody said, smiling and turning around. "You think these beasts are still around? I'm pretty sure they died out about ten thousand years ago."

"No, not that," Sam said. "But let's just say I've recently been in some secret chambers and long lost sites like this, and have found out the hard way that there are booby traps."

"You managed to get through OK," Cody said.

"I had help," Sam replied. "In Brazil, we had the benefit of a journal, written by a friend's godfather, an archaeologist who specializes in the last 13 lore."

Cody nodded and stepped aside. "How about you lead?" he offered.

They laughed.

"Sure," Sam replied, full of bravado. "Follow me. And we go *slow*."

"Next thing you'll tell me not to touch anything," Cody joked.

"That's probably good advice." Sam stopped at the threshold. Beyond the small entry door darkness loomed. "Wait a sec."

Sam looked at the worn inscriptions on the doorway, which included a carving of twelve soldiers marching. "Can I use your phone?"

"Sure," Cody said. "Reception is patchy down here, though."

Sam took the phone and called the Academy and asked to be put through to Jedi. The line sounded like it had gone dead and Sam was just about to hang up when Jedi answered.

"Jedi, it's Sam. Can you hear me?"

"Sam!" Jedi replied. "I can hear you—just. Where are you?"

"I'm going to message you pictures from a temple. We're about to go in to search for the next Gear."

"Shoot them though, I'll have Betsy II crunch them, see what we can find."

"OK, hang on the line," Sam said, and snapped a couple of photos on the phone and sent them through.

"So how's Betsy II?" Sam said, while they waited for the photos to load.

"Oh, you know . . . she's a bit more temperamental than the original Betsy, but I can't complain. It's just nice to be up and running again. How's the new Dreamer?" Jedi asked.

"All good. Why?" Sam replied.

"It's just that Lora ca—hang on," Jedi said, "images coming through. OK, we've got an 81% match. They're Olmec—but the carving of those twelve armed dudes depicts the twelve Hittite Gods of the Underworld . . . hmm, strange, wrong part of the world, I would have thought. Sure you're not in a museum, pulling my leg?"

"I'm not, I promise. But thanks," Sam said. "So, what were you saying about Lora?"

"Oh, right," Jedi said. "You're not on speakerphone, are you?"

"No."

"I'm sure it's nothing, but Lora says to keep your wits about, she's not su—"

The line went dead.

"Hello? Jedi, can you hear me?" Sam said loudly.

"What did he say?" Cody asked as Sam handed him back his phone.

"Jedi said a match came up with an Olmec carving of the twelve Hittites, Gods of the Underworld, I think he said, but the line was pretty rough."

"Olmec *and* Hittite?" Cody said, skeptical. "It can't be, not here. Anything else?"

Sam shook his head, still thinking about the last thing Jedi said.

Lora said to keep my wits about me.

"Look, we came for the Gear," Sam said, looking behind him. "So how about we go find it? Where are those skeletons?"

"Yeah, about that . . ." Cody said, not seeming to register Sam's concern. He checked that his helmet light was still on. "Get ready for darkness like you've never experienced."

Sam followed Cody through the doorway and into the inky blackness of the temple proper.

"What's that noise?" Sam whispered. He fought the urge to panic.

Nothing's wrong. Yet.

They stopped and listened. Again it came, louder this time. Like a high-pitched screaming, then—

Bats.

Thousands of them.

A cloud as thick as a storm front rolled around the corner as Sam and Cody dropped to the floor of the cave. They cowered down and huddled as the flapping wings of the tiny mammals rushed by at great speed.

"That was awesome!" Sam said after they'd passed.

"Yeah! Hey, feel that?" Cody asked.

Sam could feel a cool breeze blowing against his face from the direction of the darkness ahead. "Where's that coming from?" he asked. "Is there another entrance?"

"Maybe. But I found out the hard way what's in front of us now. Follow me. *Carefully.*"

After a few twists and turns down into the labyrinth of the cave, they came across an underground river, its black water roiling in the darkness.

"How do we cross?" Sam said, then stopped in front of a steel frame bolted into the rock floor, a cable disappearing into the fathomless void. He suddenly remembered his dream again. "Wow—the zip line. Cody, I thought you said this site was untouched, and had been for about five hundred years. So who set this up?"

"Uh, I really don't know . . ."

"And look at all these footprints! At least two sets aside from ours."

"Come on," Cody said, his voice urgent. "We have to hurry."

Sam whizzed through the air. Cody's headlamp light was a pinprick in the distance, glowing brighter as he neared.

"Squeeze the breaks," Cody instructed over their helmet intercom.

Sam squeezed the handle and slowed until he bumped into Cody at the other end. He swayed and rocked in his harness on the end of the zip line.

"OK," Sam said, unhitching himself. "We have to be quiet. Someone could still be in here."

Sam looked around the immediate area. By the beams of the flashlights, Sam could make out the scene that he'd dreamed about—but his dream didn't do this place justice. Built into this enormous carved cavern, with massive sculpted pillars supporting the roof, was a majestic, sweeping temple, complete with terraces, shrines and altars, ornate alcoves and niches, stretching away from them into the dark.

"Where'd you find those Spanish skeletons?" asked Sam.

"This way," Cody said, and they walked along the stone

ledge that formed the riverbank. The floor of the cavern was solid rock and Sam couldn't make out any footprints on this side.

Maybe they've gone the other way to explore—

"Shh!" Sam said, catching Cody by the arm to keep him still. "Listen!"

They remained still for a few minutes, listening.

"What am I listening for?" Cody whispered, finally breaking the silence.

"I heard voices."

"Maybe they're in your head, because I don't hear—"

"Look out!" Sam pulled Cody into the shadows and they flicked off their headlamps.

In front of them, the darkness was slowly being illuminated by powerful spotlights.

Then, clearly cutting through the eerie silence, the voices came again.

"Sam . . ."

"Shh!" Sam said, peering out as two headlamps came into view, getting closer and closer to where he and Cody crouched. Sam couldn't quite make out what they were saying.

"Sam—"

"*Shh!*"

Cody pushed past Sam and stepped into the light.

"Cody! What are you doing?" he hissed in disbelief. Cody started to walk towards the sound of the voices.

"It's OK, Sam," Cody called. "I know them."

Sam hesitated and then flicked on his light and followed Cody. He stopped at the sight of Cody hugging the two figures. As Sam cautiously approached, he could see their smiling faces.

"Good work, son," a man said to Cody. "This must be Sam."

Sam looked from the man to Cody, whose face couldn't hide his shame. The hum of a generator whirred into life and massive halogen lights flickered on, lighting up the underground chamber to reveal the vast extent of the temple.

"Sam, I'm Vern," the man said. He walked over and extended a gloved hand. He was wearing caving gear, like he'd come down here for a purpose—*to search.* "And this is Kate."

Sam ignored the offered handshake and watched as Kate walked up to them from the generator.

"Cody, what's going on?" Sam asked.

He didn't answer.

"Sam," Vern said. "We're Cody's parents. You turning up here has undoubtedly helped our cause, and for that, we thank you."

"*Cause?*" Sam said. He narrowed his eyes. "So you're Enterprise? Surely you know the Enterprise and the Academy are working together now. We're all in this race against the forces of evil."

"Evil?" Vern laughed drily.

"Surely you know things are never as simple as good and evil?" Kate added, smiling.

She had very pale skin and big dark eyes, her appearance making Sam think of some kind of nocturnal animal.

"Maybe. But I know evil when I see it," Sam said, looking around.

I can run, wait for a chance to circle back and make it across the zip line, cut the cable from the other side . . .

"Hmm," Kate said. "Cody, what's this boy been telling you?"

Sam listened, fierce anger building inside of him, as Cody told his Agent parents *everything.* He recounted every detail of their conversations—including the two Gears Sam had in his pack.

He lied to me from the very beginning. He knew he was leading me into a trap . . .

Sam had become so accustomed to the immediate connection he had felt with every one of the last 13 Dreamers that this unexpected betrayal stung painfully.

"Gears, eh? *Really . . .*" Vern said, his eyes fixed on Sam's backpack.

"These people are not your parents, Cody," Sam said.

"Oh, he knows that," Vern said. "You see," he put an arm around Cody's shoulders and another around Kate's, the very picture of a happy family, "*we've* always been honest with each other—about Cody, about who we are, about the purpose of our lives. But we raised him and loved him as our own. We're as much a family as any other."

Some twisted family this is.

"But what about your purpose with the Enterprise?" Sam said, already sensing what the answer would be. "We're in this together now, the Academy *and* the Enterprise."

"Oh, I'd say the rules are out the window now," Kate said, taking a dart gun out from her belt. "Sorry to say this, Sam, but while we do need you, we don't need you just *now*."

Sam could see Vern hold up a cogged brass plate, and he knew what he was looking at—the next Gear.

"You knew!" Sam shouted as he stormed towards Cody. "You knew exactly where it was the whole time!"

Kate took a step in front of her son.

THWACK!

EVA

Eva waited by the helicopter which had landed on top of the canyon, above the temple. Abseiling rope lines were being wound up by the Guardians, Lora was making a call. Eva's stomach twisted in knots, and this time it wasn't because of the height, but Lora's conversation.

"Sam's gone," Lora reported down the line. "We found an empty Enterprise dart at the scene. The Grand Canyon site is deserted but an aircraft was reportedly seen leaving the area, headed north."

"What kind of aircraft?" the Professor replied over the tiny speaker.

"US military," Lora said. "It was an Osprey by the sounds of it, and Mac would be the obvious person to have access to a military-style plane."

"We have to track it, and fast," the Professor replied. "I'll make some calls to our friends in the Dreamer Council with ties to the US Government. It seems Mac has given up any last pretense of wanting to work with us—your instinct not to trust his offer of help proved to be well-founded, Lora."

Lora tried to smile reassuringly at Eva as there was a

long pause from the Professor. Eventually he spoke again, "I think Mac might be taking Sam to Bureau 13."

Lora hesitated then sighed. "Yes, unfortunately I was thinking the same thing. We can't be certain, of course, but Mac returning to his operations base is a real possibility." She bit her bottom lip and appeared nervous. Eva was puzzled.

Operations base? What is Mac planning on doing with Sam?

"You must go there," the Professor continued. "It's the only lead we have and it's too dangerous not to follow up on. I'll divert Tobias and the team there too."

"We're on our way." Lora signaled to the pilot as she and Eva climbed on board. At once the helicopter's rotors started up, spiraling dust through the air. Lora yelled over the sound into the phone, "We'll call again when we have news!" and hung up to buckle in.

"Did you say Bureau 13?"

"I'll tell you about it later," Lora replied, subtly tilting her head towards the pilot who she clearly didn't want to overhear.

"Oh, OK," Eva said. Then she leaned over to quietly speak into Lora's ear. "It's just that someone said something about Bureau 13 in my dream last night, too."

"Right." Lora's look of concentration hardened and her hands gripped tight on the edge of the seat. "That's what I was afraid of."

SAM

Sam woke to the droning sound of a plane's engine, the rhythmic movement telling him he was airborne. As he leaned over to look out of the nearest window, he saw a stubby overhead wing and huge oversized propeller. To the rear there was a sloped cargo ramp.

"Hey, Sam," Cody said, sitting down next to him.

"Get lost."

Cody stayed where he was. "How are you feeling?"

"I *was* fine, until your mom shot me with a dart," Sam replied, craning his neck to look at Cody's parents on the other side of the aircraft. They sat together casually, leaning over a notebook. He looked back out of the window. "I'm so *over* getting knocked out," he muttered.

"I'm sorry about that."

"Sure you are."

Sam continued to look out the window and wondered where they were headed. He stayed quiet, ignoring Cody's company, staring hopefully below to see something—a landmark, a city—that he would recognize.

So they aren't working with the Enterprise anymore.

It doesn't make sense for them to side with Hans . . . that leaves Stella or Mac.

"How long have we been flying?" Sam finally spoke.

"An hour I suppose . . ."

"Do you know where Vern and Kate work?" Sam asked Cody.

"You mean who they work *for*?" Cody replied.

"I suppose."

"No, I don't."

Sam rolled his eyes at Cody then craned around him to look at his parents again. They were still sitting close, reading their book. Sam looked back to Cody, who looked guilty.

"Whatever," Sam said. "Like I said before—get lost."

"OK," Cody admitted. "So I already knew about this part. And I told them the night before I met you about seeing the Gear in my dream and where they could find it. I knew they were going to be there at the site. But I had no idea that they'd dart you like that."

Sam scoffed.

"Really, I didn't. Sam, it'll be OK. My parents aren't the bad guys."

May as well try to get what I can out of him . . .

Sam asked, "Is that what Stella told you to say?"

"What? No!"

"So you've all been brainwashed by Mac's lies then, is that it?"

"He hasn't brainw—" Cody started to say, before stopping himself mid-sentence.

Aha! So Mac is behind this . . .

Sam decided to let it rest for now. He looked through furious eyes at Vern and Kate, huddled together, still reading. They seemed oblivious to the fact that Sam was awake and talking to their son.

They'll pay attention to me when they need to, as Kate said before . . .

"Wait!" Sam said suddenly, snapping out of his thoughts, "I know that notebook!" He looked in shock at the familiar cover of the book that Vern and Kate both held. "That belonged to Dr. Kader! Where did you get it?"

"A friend sent it to us," Vern said, finally looking up at Sam, but seeming unsurprised at his outburst. "It's been quite helpful, actually."

Sam could see snippets of the familiar pages across the space between them, filled with hand-drawn images and densely packed notes.

"Was it you who kidnapped Dr. Kader?" Sam asked urgently. "Do you know where he is?"

"Yes, they do," a voice said.

A figure emerged from the rear of the aircraft, his face backlit by the brilliant sun coming in through the window. Sam had to shield his eyes against the glare.

"Dr. Kader?" Sam said, still shocked. He was relieved, and ecstatic, to see the kindhearted Egyptologist safe and well. But his relief began to fade as the other possibility dawned on him. "Are you—are you working with *them?*"

As Dr. Kader came closer, Sam noticed that he held two brass Gears in his right hand. He knew the answer to his question before Dr. Kader spoke.

"Sam, *please*, call me Ahmed," Dr. Kader said. "I am here in my professional capacity. I decided that it would be beneficial to approach this situation from another vantage point."

"What—from that of a thief?" Sam said.

Ahmed shook his head.

"So you're a prisoner here too?" Sam said, desperately offering him the benefit of the doubt.

"I was persuaded to come, it's true—but for my protection. But I can honestly say, I now understand that this is indeed where I am meant to be." Dr. Kader put a hand on Sam's shoulder. "You'll realize that too, Sam, I promise."

"But—but if they," Sam said, referring to Kate and Vern, "are no longer Enterprise Agents . . ." He looked around the military aircraft, trying to piece it all together in his head. "You're working for Mac now?"

"*With*," Dr. Kader emphasized. "I work *with* Mac."

"It's a private arrangement," Kate added. "It's not an official assignment."

Vern smirked, and added, "More of a top-secret project."

"I think you mean illegal." Sam glared back at them,

before turning to Ahmed again. "But what about the Academy? What about Xavier . . . your *godson?*" Sam's voice strained at the question.

"Yes, I know, but the Academy and the Enterprise are too weak now. They can be of no use, even with your talents, against Solaris, and Stella and Hans . . ." Ahmed looked pained at what he was saying. "We are against those who fight this battle without any rules. Only the strongest have a chance of beating them."

"But Xavier," Sam repeated, "and his father—"

"Remain my dearest friends," Dr. Kader said. "And once we've succeeded in this mission, they will understand why I had to make this decision in this race and life will go back to normal."

"You think?" Sam said, defiant. "'Cause *I* think they'll see it differently. They're smart enough to see you for what you really are—nothing but a sellout."

"Maybe. Time will tell," Dr. Kader said sadly, letting out a big sigh. "I'll admit, at first, it wasn't an easy choice to make—"

"You look pretty comfortable with how things are to me," Sam interrupted, eyeing the Gears in Ahmed's hand.

"But as the days have passed," Ahmed continued undeterred, "I've come to realize I have made the right decision. This is where I am best suited."

"Working with lowlifes and liars?" Sam asked.

"No." He pointed to Cody's parents. "With the people

holding all the power, Sam. Mac's got the resources to see this race through to the finish line. You'd do well to come around to my way of thinking."

A man in army uniform came forward and announced, "We're coming in for our landing approach, time to strap in tight."

Sam shook his head at Dr. Kader, who looked sad at Sam's steadfast refusal to see things his way. He turned and walked slowly back to his seat and strapped in.

"You've stayed quiet," Sam said through his teeth to Cody. He took a few deep breaths as he strapped on his belt, trying to calm down and free himself from the overwhelming feeling of betrayal.

"Sorry," was all Cody could say in response.

It's no use being angry. Breathe, clear your head, try to think straight, and get out of this mess.

Sam looked out the window at a huge, sprawling airport that was coming into view below.

"Hey, isn't that . . ?" Cody said, his voice wavering before breaking off.

The airport from Cody's dream. Oh no . . .

33

ALEX

"Seven hundred," Alex hunched over and caught his breath. "So . . . tired . . . so . . . hungry . . ."

He thought back to the bagel that he'd dumped when he learned of his mother's disappearance and his stomach groaned.

"Least . . . I have a dart gun." In one hand, he held the gun, in the other, a flashlight which he was using to light the way. Either the power was out in the Washington Monument or he'd not found the right switch to turn the lights on in the stairwell before starting his ascent. He tried his radio but there was no reception.

"OK . . . seven hundred down," he said, resuming his trek upstairs. "Or should I say up. One hundred and ninety-seven to go. The things I have to do . . . to save the world!"

Alex paused at the last landing before the top. He stood there, listening, straining to make out any sound. At first, all seemed quiet above. He crept closer, one step at a time.

His footfalls were gentle, as silent as possible, his dart gun held out in front. The flashlight was not needed now; the floor above was illuminated from the windows at the observation deck.

He stopped at the last corner, where he remained hidden and still.

Then came the quiet murmur of voices.

At least two people.

As the minutes ticked by, they spoke about trivial things, and at first he was sure that they were just construction guys or security. But then they got a call, and although he could only hear one side of the conversation, it soon developed into full disclosure. The guy on the phone hung up and said to his colleague, "We have to keep a lookout, one of those Enterprise guys is still out there, dressed as a DC cop."

"Enterprise punks," the other said. "They should have sided with us. Come on, let's get out there and wire in this capstone."

So Alex waited, and it took another ten minutes for them to talk and mutter and, he imagined, slip into climbing harnesses. He could hear them climb out of the maintenance windows onto the sloping side of the pyramidion capstone.

Alex ventured out to the observation area. It was deserted.

Big, heavy steel doors at the back of the elevator shaft

were open, revealing a maze of wires that snaked up to the capstone and down to the ground floor. There was no telling which wire was for what. The elevator, PA system, smoke detectors, observation deck lighting and the aircraft warning beacon would all have wires coming down here.

No way can I cut through all these. It'd take too long and I'd probably electrocute myself in the bargain.

There were open toolboxes on the ground.

And a gun.

A big, mean-looking assault rifle. He picked it up and felt the heavy weight of it. With a bit of fiddling he managed to eject the magazine. It was full of bullets—real, live bullets.

Stella's goons? Maybe Mac's? Or someone else completely. That Hans dude? Man, either way, they're the enemy.

He emptied the bullets out of the magazine, dropping them down the void near the wires, and put the rifle back how he'd found it. Then he went through an open door, marked:

RESTRICTED ACCESS

OFFICIAL PERSONNEL ONLY.

Looking up into the space between the inner and outer stone layers, Alex saw that it was light in there—lit up by lamps and blowing a gale—they definitely had the maintenance hatch open, and with luck they were both already outside.

Soon to be trapped out there . . .

Alex took the steel ladder up and waited on the gangway that led out to the hatch near the very top of the pyramid. The hatch opened inward.

Great, I can just lock them out there.

But as he reached up to the hatch, he heard one of them call out. "That's it, we're done. Let's get out of here."

Time to act fast!

There was a lot less time than he thought.

One of the guys came through the hatch, legs first, and when he landed on his feet, he turned to look straight at Alex, eyes wide—

PFFT! PFFT!

The first dart hit him in the leg. The second, as Alex took careful aim, hit him point-blank in the neck. The man slumped forward and landed heavily on the walkway, out cold.

"Don't move!" Alex shouted as the next guy went to make the same entry, seemingly oblivious to his comrade's fate. "I'm armed! Come through, slowly!"

The guy shuffled through and jumped down in front of Alex. He looked down and saw his friend knocked out cold.

"Put your hands on your head!" Alex commanded.

The man did so. He was still roped in to his climbing harness and anchored to the metal rails on the walkway. The guy was twice Alex's age and at least twice his bulk. And he was wearing the uniform of a US Marine.

"Who do you work for?" Alex asked.

At first, it seemed like the guy wasn't going to answer, but then Alex gave an indication with his pistol and it was enough to get the man talking.

"Isn't it obvious?" the man replied, then reeled off his name, rank and serial number.

"OK," Alex said. "But something tells me you're not on official business. Who's your 'commanding officer' now?"

The Marine didn't answer.

Alex said, "Let's assume that his name is Mac." There was a reaction in the guy's face and Alex could tell that he was on the money. "OK, you're a Marine, so you're used to following orders. Now you're going to do exactly as *I* say . . ."

34

SAM

The rain was starting to fall hard. Sam couldn't see exactly where they were, but he did have the familiar dèjá vu feeling that came with living out a dream.

The airport . . . is this the place where Solaris shows up?

The aircraft had touched down and taxied to the hangar. Everything from that point had happened so fast that Sam felt as though he really *was* inside a dream—watching it skip by in playback—detached, like a spectator.

"This way," Vern said, and the five of them piled into the back of a van. They began a drive along the fringe of the massive airport, headed for the main terminals.

Sam had butterflies in his stomach as they drove. He could tell that Cody did too. Dr. Kader sat silently, avoiding eye contact with everyone.

"There's a storm coming," Sam said, looking at the black clouds rolling across the mountain tops. "Big one." As he spoke, a flash of lightning crackled above them.

"We're not going to wait around out here to experience it," Kate snapped.

Cody sat next to Sam in the back row of the van. He

was looking increasingly uneasy—not at all like the care-free adventurer that Sam had met just the day before. Sam knew that it wasn't the weather that was making him look so uncomfortable.

Welcome to the real adventure, Cody.

"Did you tell your mom and dad about this part of your dream?" Sam asked Cody quietly as they drove across the tarmac. "It's funny, you don't look so sure of things now."

Cody didn't respond, he just stared wide-eyed out the window.

"Why are we here?" Sam asked.

"It's our base," Kate replied.

Sam looked around—the huge terminal buildings, the flashing lights of dozens of aircraft coming and going. "At an airport?"

"Under it." The look she gave indicated that she was not going to provide any more information.

"This site is known as Central Ark." Dr. Kader turned around from the middle row of seats to face Sam. "A place where the country's leaders can flee to in the event of a catastrophe. There are other refuges on the East and West coasts too."

"And why are we here?"

"It has another purpose," Dr. Kader said. "It's one of the country's most secret sites."

"Oh yeah?" Sam tried hard to sound uninterested but

the chance to discover information that could help them in the race was tempting.

"There's another part of the site, known as Bureau 13. And I'm told that it's Mac's operations center for his own Dreamer research. Once this was linked to the government program, but as you have discovered, it's now run more . . . privately. Off the record, so to speak."

Cody's phone bleeped.

Sam, we r all headed 2 denver airport. Reply if received.

"It's for you," Cody said, showing Sam.

Sam smiled. "Lora knows where we are."

"She's too late," Vern said. "Sam, care to tell her that you're OK and need to lay low for 24 hours?"

"How about *no?*"

"Very well," Vern said.

As they drove on, something caught Sam's eye through the sheets of rain. He turned to Cody who had noticed it too. A huge statue of a black stallion, rearing up, loomed ahead, its glowing eyes burning bright red through the dreary light.

"Whoa . . ." Cody was transfixed, and he met Sam's gaze once they'd passed by. "My dream—it's happening."

Sam said, "I know."

"Which means—"

"We're not alone."

"Right." Cody seemed to turn a paler shade of white. "Solaris comes here."

Sam nodded.

"Is that true?" Dr. Kader asked.

Both Sam and Cody nodded.

"Fascinating," Dr. Kader's voice trailed off in wonder.

"Well, I think we'll be able to deal with him," Vern said smugly from the front of the van. They drove through a guarded checkpoint and then down a ramp which wound in a wide circle to where a roller door opened. Beyond the door they followed a couple of twists and turns, ending in a military roadblock. "This is one of the most secure places in the world. Solaris would need quite an army to trouble these guys."

Sam saw two tanks sitting imposingly on either side of the entrance, the road continuing through to a parking lot full of black vehicles, all with tinted windows. Uniformed soldiers patrolled the area.

"This is it," their driver said, and all the occupants of the van poured out and walked to a steel blast door that opened as they neared. Sam and Cody were at the end of the line. They had their photographs taken and identification passes were handed across the desk almost immediately.

"Don't suppose I can have my Gears back now?" Sam asked Dr. Kader as they stood in an elevator that gathered speed as it took them far underground.

"I'm sorry, Sam," Dr. Kader replied as the elevator doors finally opened. "We need them for a while yet for further study of the good Mr. da Vinci."

"You're still going on about the da Vinci theory?" Kate said as she waited for them all to alight and then fell to the back of the group as they were ushered down a corridor.

"What do you mean theory?" Sam asked, but she didn't answer him.

They walked past heavy doors labeled with various warnings—Hazardous material level V: Shanti Virus; DHARMA-cleared persons only beyond this point; Warning: high concentrations of tachyons present; Theterium processing room.

The group stopped at a door simply labeled:

Their two army escorts stayed put at the door and Vern led the way, holding the door open for the others to enter.

"Greetings! Welcome, everyone." Among the screens and lab equipment, standing in the middle of all the technicians and analysts scurrying around, was Mac.

EVA

Eva said, "Sam's being held at Denver International Airport?"

"Under it," Lora replied from her seat in the back of the chopper. "The government has a secret site underneath the airport."

"What *is* it with all this Dreamer stuff being underground?" Eva asked.

"It's safe, secure—secret," Lora replied. "It allows people to operate in their own little world."

"Kinda like dreaming, huh?" Eva looked out the window. "OK, tell me about this secret place."

"Well, to start with, I spent a lot of my life in Colorado," Lora said. "Couple of small towns, then did my first three years of college in Denver. I could have gone anywhere, but I was drawn there."

"As a Dreamer?"

"Yes. I had recurring dreams that I had to go there, to live there. It was the weirdest three years of my life."

"Well, it *is* Denver . . ."

They laughed.

"Not just that," Lora said. "You ever passed through Denver International Airport?"

"No."

"Well, try this for size," Lora said. "An apocalyptic horse with glowing red eyes welcoming visitors? *Check.* Nightmarish murals? *Check.* Strange words and symbols embedded in the floor? *Check.* Full of occult symbolism and references to secret societies. *Check.* The truth is, the whole place is one big cover for what's underneath."

"Which is?" Eva was starting to feel freaked out.

"Two things. First came Bureau 13. That was then expanded to include the Central Ark."

"The what?"

"One of three places in the country where people in the know can hide in the event of a full-scale disaster—a kind of gigantic storm shelter."

"How gigantic?"

"Denver is the largest airport in America. Underneath, its Ark is the newest of the three in this country. I've heard it can house 500,000 people for up to ten years. We only know of it through the Professor's contacts on the Dreamer Council."

"Wow."

"And it's also where Mac could be trying to control the prophecy of the last 13."

"**S**am," Mac said. "So nice to see you again."

"Why am I even surprised to see you here?" Sam asked.

"Well, I do run this show," Mac said with a smile appearing under his thick moustache. "And, I assure you, it's the greatest show on earth!"

Sam noticed one of the big screens behind Mac showed overhead footage of the Academy's campus outside London. He glanced at another which showed—*my parents!*

Sam struggled to control his emotions and make his face impassive as he watched footage of the two of them and his little brother eating at a family restaurant, oblivious to the long-lens camera trained on them at that very moment.

Are they in danger? Why is Mac watching them? Why aren't they looking for me?

Too many thoughts crowded into Sam's mind at once. He shook his head, trying to regain his focus.

"I will go and analyze the Gears," Dr. Kader said, and excused himself from the room.

Mac gave a wave and a couple of guards shadowed the archaeologist out.

Sam stole a glance at his "family," trying to remind himself who they really were.

Where are they now? Are they working with Mac? Against me? Do they miss me? Do they care—really care?

All those nights his dad had driven him to jujitsu practice. All those times they'd gone on family adventures, all the dinners, all the fun times.

Wherever they are, I'm going to find them. Find them and see for myself.

"You're no soldier, you've got no code of conduct, do you?" Sam said to Mac. He looked to Cody's parents, who looked unfazed by the comment. "Do you two know this guy, I mean, *really* know him? Do you trust him?"

"Sam, why don't you have a rest?" Mac said. "You look tired. We have some comfortable rooms here, and I'm sure you'll have *wonderful* dreams."

Dreams that he'll mine for every detail.

"Cody," Sam said, "this guy, he may be their boss as the head of Bureau 13, but he has no intention of using the true dreams for the good of the country or the world. He wants it for himself. He just wants the power at the end of it all, that ultimate power from the prophecy—"

"Enough!" Mac shouted suddenly.

"You're double agents, right?" Sam said to Cody's parents, ignoring Mac's interjection. "You're here because you think you're doing the right thing for your country—but you don't *know* this guy!"

Vern and Kate looked to one another, the slightest bit of doubt creeping into their minds.

"Cody," Sam said quickly before Mac could cut him off. "How'd your parents know that you were having your dreams?"

Cody looked from Sam to his parents, and his expression slowly changed, as did theirs. The truth was coming out.

"How *did* you know?" Cody asked them.

"Your journal." Vern looked to the floor after admitting that.

"You read my dream journal?" Cody said, surprised. "That was meant to be private!"

"Son, the stakes are too high—"

"Be quiet!" Mac shouted.

"No!" Sam shouted back. He turned to Cody's parents desperately. "You guys don't know the real Mac! What he's capable of!"

"Enough!" Mac stormed, striding across the room.

"Cody," Kate said, "the Enterprise took over the government's work in the genetic development of Dreamers when those in Washington got too squeamish. But they've always had a hand in things. They've always watched, waited."

"Why?" Cody asked.

"Because they want the Dream Gate for themselves,"

Sam replied.

"True," Kate said. "It cannot fall into anyone else's hands."

"America must have this power to control," Vern added.

"It's for the whole *world*. We should share this," Sam said. "But not with this man involved. He wants it for himself—not the country."

Vern looked at Mac suspiciously.

"That's not for you or us to decide," Kate said. "I mean, we're just following orders—"

"The orders of a madman!" Sam said, then Mac snapped altogether.

"Take him away! Get him out of here!" he shouted, and two huge Marines came forward and grabbed Sam by the arms.

"What are you going to do with me?" Sam asked.

"You'll find out soon enough," Mac sneered.

"And Cody?"

Mac looked from Sam to Cody's parents, who both appeared for the first time to be truly questioning this man.

"What happens with Cody?" Vern asked Mac.

"Oh, you believe *him* now?" Mac said, a crooked finger pointed at Sam. "Look at your own *parents*, Sam, look at that screen."

Sam looked, the Marines still holding him.

"We've been watching them," Mac said, "thinking that you might turn up there for a little reunion."

Sam watched as older footage of his surrogate parents played out on other screens.

It's almost as if they don't miss me.

But then he saw that they did. His mother's face looked . . .

"I can bring them in, or take you to them, if you like," Mac said, interrupting Sam's thoughts. "Whatever you want. But you have to come around to *my* way of thinking. You have to see that what I'm doing is the *right thing.* Join me, Sam. Before it's too late."

Sam shook his head.

"Mac, maybe we need to talk about all this," Vern said. "Away from the boys—"

"Take them all away!" Mac said, and Marines rushed at Cody and his parents.

"You fools!" Mac said as Vern tried to fight his way out but was quickly overpowered. "What's happening here is bigger than all of you—it's bigger than *anything* you could ever imagine!"

"Look at Mac's eyes," Sam said. "See that wild look? Does he look like a guy that's gonna say one thing and do another?"

"That's right, Sam!" Mac admitted. "I answer to no one, not my government, and certainly not *your* Dreamer Council. No one understands the power of the Dream Gate. Only one gets to enter, don't you see? That's always been understood about the prophecy. And you think I'm going to let that person be *you?* Or the *President?* Or the *Professor?*

Or—or *Solaris?*" Mac laughed. "It's going to be me!" he said, his eyes maniacal. "I *alone* will wield the power beyond the Gate!"

Sam looked to Cody's parents, willing them, now that they too were captive, to come around and see things for what they really were.

"Wait!" Vern said, looking directly at Mac as two Marines held his arms. "What are you going to do with Sam, with Cody?"

"These two?" Mac said. "We're going to unlock Sam's genetic code, see where it all went right. First to discover all that he knows and will dream in the coming days, and then to make more Dreamers like him."

"And Cody?"

Mac smiled. "He's served his purpose and is now US government property," Mac said. "I'd say they'll be studying him for a while to come. Studying him, while I continue on to the Dream Gate, ha!"

Cody's parents struggled against their Marine captors, his mother now yelling and pushing to break free. But it was no use.

"Sam," Mac said, his voice calm once more, confident he had the upper hand. "It really doesn't have to be this way. I'm happy to have you share in what we're doing here, in our research into the Dream Gate." He pointed at a technician who replaced the screens showing Sam's parents with overhead shots of Egypt. "A while ago we found two undiscovered pyramids in Egypt. And here, we've found sites in Saudi Arabia. And this, in Antarctica, and in Russia."

Sam looked at all the images playing on the screen, then said, "So?"

"So, Sam," Mac said. "We're unlocking all the secrets of the past with you and your dreams. This is bigger than anything the Professor and the Dreamer Council, or even the director of the Enterprise has ever imagined. This is so much more than world *changing*. In the wrong hands, it's world *ending*."

"Who, in your eyes, are the wrong hands?" Sam asked.

"Anyone but me."

"You're crazy," Sam said. "I'll never, ever, side with you."

"You'll come to see that what we're doing is right. You'll see."

Sam said, "Whatever is beyond the Gate needs to be shared."

"By who, the Professor and the Academy? The Council of Dreamers?" Mac said. "We all answer to someone. And I think the American people know best."

"The American people?" Cody said. "Whatever treasure and secrets lie beyond the Dream Gate, it's just going to be locked away in this vault, never seen again. It belongs to us all!"

"You have no idea of the ramifications—" Mac said.

"You'll never be able to keep it locked away," Sam said,

his voice quiet. "We'll find it."

"Sorry?" Mac said.

"The Gears, the Dream Gate," Sam said. "You don't know how we 13 dream when we're around them. And it's not just me and Cody, there are others."

"Oh, believe me, I know . . ." Mac said, the maniacal expression back on his face.

"You may get a step ahead of the others," Sam said, "but you won't be able to stop Solaris."

The lights in the bunker flickered, and then all the screens in the room went off. The lights too.

The emergency lighting blinked on. A siren began screeching somewhere.

Sam smiled.

Maybe right now the enemy of my enemy is my friend.

"It's too late!" he said over the noise. "He's here!"

37

EVA

Lora and Eva's helicopter was forced to land well short of the airport.

"Oh no . . ." Lora said.

"What is this?" Eva asked.

"The flight space around Denver is shut down," the pilot said.

"Why?" Lora asked.

"No idea," the pilot replied. "But orders are orders. We wait here until the airspace is cleared."

"They're evacuating the city," Lora said, reading a news update from her phone. "Some kind of emergency procedure at the power plant."

"What?" Eva said.

"It's Mac," Lora said, not believing the news report. "It has to be."

"How can he evacuate a city?"

"Because he's working for the government—or at least, they think he is."

First Stella, then Hans and Mac. Now the US government is against us. And if they want the Dream Gate, other world powers will too. Things just got a whole lot more complicated.

"How do we get to Sam?" Eva asked.

"We go back," Lora replied.

"Back?"

Lora called Jedi, and when he answered she said, "Jedi, I need eyes on Mount Blanca."

"On it," he replied.

"There's another way into Bureau 13." Lora punched the name of Alamosa County into the GPS on her tablet. "Via Mount Blanca—it's a huge mountain surrounding the San Luis Valley here in Southern Colorado. Not far from here."

"What's there?" Eva asked.

"A secret military underground base at the foot of the mountain, built into the lava tubes that run all the way up to Denver," Jedi said. "There are supposed to be underground waterfalls there bigger than Niagara. A very interesting place, and more importantly, for us, it's linked underground to the Bureau 13 site via their emergency evac protocols."

"We're headed there now," Lora said, and showed the pilots their new destination. "Have you heard about road closures into Denver?"

"It's all over the news," Jedi said.

"What is it?" Lora said.

"Authorities won't say, but it's suspected to be a nuclear accident at one of the weapons plants there."

"Got those pictures yet?" Lora asked.

"Coming through now," Jedi replied, and the image of his face was replaced with overhead real-time shots from Mount Blanca. "This place has been mothballed, ever since it first opened."

"I don't get it. Why?" Eva asked as the helicopter took off again.

"It was always intended to be a backup site," Lora explained. "It needed to be ready but with just a skeleton crew to keep things secure and working, that's it."

"Something's not right . . ." Jedi said. "There's not even a skeleton crew. There's nothing."

"What is it?" Eva asked.

"We're not the first ones to think of it, obviously . . ." the image zoomed in. Guards were lying on the ground at the security gates, out for the count.

"This place doesn't look mothballed anymore," Lora said.

"I agree," Jedi said. "Proceed with maximum caution."

"We'd better get there as quick as we can," Lora said. "Eva, buckle up tight."

SAM

"You'll dream forever, and we'll be getting each and every dream," Mac said.

"I don't think so," Sam said. "My friends will come for me!"

Mac smiled and pointed to a clock counting down on the wall:

"In less than an hour," he said, "a small nuclear device built into this complex will be detonated. Your friends will be mourning your death, and we will be a long way away."

"But you'll kill everyone in the city above!" Sam said.

"It's being evacuated as we speak," Mac replied. "Sold as a leak from the local nuclear plant. Don't worry, this will hurt nothing but your precious loyalty."

"You'll never evacuate everyone in time!"

"There may be a few casualties of war," Mac replied.

"You're mad!" Sam yelled.

"Quite the contrary, Sam. I'm a *genius*."

"You'll never get away with this. And you'll never get my dreams from me. I'll hold out."

58:56

58:55

58:54

"I don't think so," Mac said. "You see, Sam, I helped to create you. I was involved with the DNA sequencing and the discovery of the Dreamer Gene."

Sam stopped straining against the straps.

58:42

"At least warn Lora and the Academy team not to try and rescue me."

"They control their own destiny," Mac said casually.

"But killing innocent people?"

"If Lora knows you are here, then Solaris will, and probably Stella and Hans too," Mac said. "It's a move we have to make to ensure that we are left to do our work."

"Work?"

"You will dream, Sam, hard and fast."

"*You're* dreaming," Sam said. "The dreams of a madman."

Mac smiled. "We have ways, you know. Hard, *painful* ways. Make it easy on yourself—you dream of the next six Dreamers, and with our guidance I think we will be able to do that in, oh, forty-eight hours. Dream of them, we get the remaining Gears, and we hold the power to unlock the Dream Gate. You can stop anyone else getting hurt, Sam. If that's what means most to you."

"You're forgetting that some of the Gears are in other people's hands."

"A small matter that our operatives in the field will remedy," Mac replied.

"Solaris has one," Sam said.

Suddenly a louder alarm sounded and red lights flashed above.

Mac finally looked startled.

Sam couldn't help but smile.

At last, something's not going to plan.

"What is it?" Mac asked an aide, who got on a phone and then said, "Sir, there's been a security breach. All our cameras are down, but we've had radio reports of an intruder in a black suit that resembles our stolen dream-flage suit."

"Solaris!" Mac said, grinning. "That's how he's getting into the last 13's dreams! Where is he?"

"Inside the complex, the east wing."

Mac looked pleased. "Excellent . . . keep tracking him and form a welcoming party."

ALEX

"Alex, are you OK?" Phoebe asked.

"I'm fine, Mom," Alex said, catching his breath.

This trade had better work.

"Mom?" the Marine sniggered.

"Shut up, fool," Alex said to him. He stood with the empty assault rifle pointed at the Marine, having just bound his wrists behind his back with electrical tape, his darted buddy unconscious by his feet.

Across the room at the base of the Washington Monument, four soldiers stood guard over the dozen Enterprise Agents they'd captured, along with Phoebe.

"Untie them and send them over," Alex commanded.

The Marines did so, the Agents crossing quickly to Alex. He passed his dart gun to his mother, along with the Marine's phone.

"How'd you find us?" Phoebe asked.

"I asked this guy nicely as we walked down from the top of the Monument and he carried his unconscious friend," Alex replied. "Oh, and I, ah, disconnected the wires. For good."

"Disconnected?" Phoebe said.

"Yeah, I actually, um, well, I should probably apologize to America sometime soon."

His mother looked puzzled.

"Here," Alex said, cutting the Marine's ties and letting him drag his comrade with him. "And next time," Alex called out, "be man enough to question your superior officer when it comes to actions against your own civilian population!"

The Marine gave him a final, filthy glance.

"That goes for the rest of you too!" Alex called out as the group of Marines retreated. He passed the assault rifle to one of the Enterprise Agents, who kept it trained on the soldiers. "It's not loaded," he whispered to him.

"Come on," Phoebe said. "I just called in, the director's up at the Mall with a small army of Agents and Guardians."

They rushed up to the surface, and raced across to the rendezvous point at the side of the National Museum of American History.

"Over here!" the director called, standing by a convoy of blacked-out SUVs.

There were several police cars acting as escort, though Alex wasn't sure if they were real cops or Agents in disguise. Either way, it was an impressive looking turnout.

"But how did you take care of the Monument?" he asked.

Alex pointed to where the heavy aluminum capstone had smashed deep into the pavement outside the Monument.

"Kinda used some of the Marine's explosives," Alex said. "I thought it might just damage it—the wires. But I guess I used too much. I blew the capstone off like a rocket!" He could barely suppress a sheepish laugh.

"Excellent work! Destructive, but effective," the director said, clearly pleased with the result. "Let's move, we have no time to lose."

"What is it?" Phoebe asked as they piled into the cars.

"It's Sam, and the next Dreamer," the director replied.

Alex's heart skipped a beat. "What about them?"

"They're at the old Bureau 13 headquarters, in Denver," he said. "And the city is being evacuated. There's been a nuclear fallout threat."

The convoy was already underway, speeding through the streets, the way ahead cleared thanks to the cop cars.

"How long do they have?" Alex asked.

The director looked grim as he replied, "Not long enough."

SAM

57:42
Sam looked at the others in the room, still being held tight by Marines. He knew that they too were scared, and that they now realized that this man, Mac, was certainly *not* working in the best interests of any country.

57:34

"Finally," Mac said, rubbing his hands together like a giddy child. "I can't *wait* to see who's behind that mask."

"He's already breached sector seven, sir," a Marine called out.

"Then grab all the security you can find and follow me," Mac said, leaving Sam and the others alone in the control room. The technicians hesitated only a moment, then fled the room, not eager to remain to find out the cause of the alarm.

Stolen dream-flage suit?

Sam thought about it.

Is that how he can enter other people's dreams?

A loud blast echoed from the corridor where Mac had just headed.

"Keep an eye on them!" the Marine in charge said, leaving just one soldier to guard Sam and the others. He drew his pistol to warn them to comply.

56:17

Another booming blast came from outside the door, this one closer, and the soldier instinctively turned to the sound—

It was all the time Sam needed. He threw himself at the soldier, forcing the gun from his hand and knocking him out with two fluid jujitsu moves. He bent down to scoop up the gun as—

PFFT! PFFT! PFFT!

"Sam . . ."

That voice. Electrifying, horrifying.

Solaris.

Sam turned and looked up. That's when he realized something was different.

Solaris was dressed in what looked like an armored suit. The voice remained the same but the vision was even more terrifying.

Sam looked for Cody and his parents, but they were on the ground—passed out—darts sticking out of their chests like feathered daggers.

"Don't, Sam," Solaris said, his hand outstretched with the lanyard holding the three Gears, as if offering them to him.

Sam realized he had the gun pointed at Solaris' face.

"Why shouldn't I?" Sam asked. "You're a ruthless villain."

"Thank you." He continued to hold out the Gears and Sam reached forward tentatively and snatched them from Solaris' grasp, pulling back immediately.

"What are you doing?" Sam asked, slipping them over his neck.

"If they get you," Solaris said, "we all lose."

"So what, we work together now? You think we're going to be some kind of team?"

Solaris stared at him. It was impossible to know what was going on behind that mask, but Sam almost thought that he sensed a smile.

"You'll keep, Sam," Solaris said, as the world around them started to fill with pieces of dust and smoke as Mac's men returned, shooting their way back into the room.

"What do we do?" Sam said.

"We leave," Solaris said, then moved to a panel with a key in it—where Mac had switched on the nuclear charge.

Solaris turned the key.

The countdown clicked over from *52:55* to—

05:59

"*No!*" Sam cried.

05:58

05:57

05:56